ROY LEWIS

Seek For Justice

COLLINS, ST JAMES'S PLACE, LONDON

William Collins Sons & Co. Ltd
London · Glasgow · Sydney · Auckland
Toronto · Johannesburg

First published 1981
© Roy Lewis, 1981

British Library Cataloguing in Publication Data
Lewis, Roy, *1933*—
    Seek for justice. —(Crime Club)
    I. Title
    823'.914 [F]   PR6062.E954
    ISBN 0 00 231872 5

Photoset in Compugraphic Baskerville
Printed in Great Britain by
T. J. Press (Padstow) Ltd

F

What is done, is done:
Spend not the time in tears, but seek for justice.

John Ford: *'Tis Pity She's a Whore*

CHAPTER 1

I

In the hot morning sunshine the valley floor shimmered
and moved, dancing lights reflecting from the slow
quiescence of the once black river, the grey-green of the
hillsides still in the airless hush. Across the valley the
mountain rose against a backdrop of sharp blue sky, its
steep slopes now shaded with plantations of fir trees he
had not known as a boy, but here, below him and nearer
to hand, the road was as he remembered it, looping, ribboning downward in a series of sharp bends, doubling
back on itself in several hairpins, until it levelled out in
the long straight run beyond the reservoir, past the twin
collieries of the Parc and the Dare.

He could recall the feel of the wind in his face as he had
ridden down that stretch of road on a bicycle, with Jeff
far behind him. It was a thought he did not want to dwell
upon.

Alan Fearnley turned, and walked away from the car,
and the valley was at his back as he strolled aimlessly
along the mountain road. In a few minutes he was at the
other side of the hill, looking down towards Llantrisant,
and the trees were thick now, a heavy green carpet
bordering the road as it ran whitely down towards the
vale and the distant sea. He stood there, staring, and a
light breeze rose, whispering at his back. It was time to
go; in an hour or so they'd be burying his brother.

When he drove down over the Bwlch-y-Clawdd he did so
slowly, and carefully. The road ran straight for perhaps
three hundred yards, then swung sharply into a left-hand

bend. To his right, a line of white-painted stones marked the edge of the road, but no barrier existed between the car and a plunge down over the grassy slopes to the little cwm below. He stayed in third gear as he passed the narrow lay-by constructed under the overhang of grey, harsh rock, and drove slowly into the second curving left-hander that followed the shoulder of the mountain, placing his back to the valley again, heading into the wide basin of the hills ahead of him. His mouth was suddenly dry, and he stared ahead fixedly: two hundred yards, and there was the grey stone wall that overlooked the reservoir far below. A right-hand hairpin would swing him past and above the reservoir; he would then straighten out and coast past the collieries, down into the villages that threaded the valley floor.

He slowed at the hairpin, braking, and he saw the broken fence, gaps yawning widely still where Jeff's car had crashed through, bounding high with the impact and lurching, roaring, up into the void beyond the fence. Its wheels would have been spinning crazily as it hit the rocky slope, to somersault in the death-dive beyond.

Alan drove into the hairpin, went on for a hundred yards and then stopped. It was several minutes before he could bring himself to leave the car, but he knew he had to do it. He pulled himself together, and walked back to the hairpin, and the broken fence. The sun was hot on the back of his neck as he stared down the hillside.

The water of the reservoir was blue and deep and still. Sheep grazed aimlessly on the hummocky grass of the slope but Alan's glance was riveted to the scars the tractors had made across the hillside, when they had come up through the bare slopes of the cwm to haul away the burned-out vehicle in which Jeff had died. In time those scars would heal, the wounds disappearing under the fast-growing grass. But they would still be there, gouged out of the earth.

Men could be like that: scarred, but hiding their scars behind growing experiences and acceptances. Until, from time to time, someone stripped away the protective coverings and the damage was exposed again.

He went back to the car quickly, and drove down into the village. There was a café in the main street where he had often gone with his friends, run by the inevitable Welsh-accented Italian and the incomprehensible wife he had been sent from southern Italy. Alan parked in a side street and went there now; it was smaller than he remembered, and dingier, and the girl behind the counter would be one of the daughters and unknown to him, but it was still fifteen minutes to the service and he had no desire to arrive at the church too soon.

He timed it to his satisfaction. After he had finished his espresso coffee it was a short walk to the Catholic church, and he was the last to arrive. The usher looked at him oddly, as though he knew him, but directed him, nevertheless, to the left-hand side of the small church, with the friends of the deceased, rather than beside his relatives, to the right. Alan made no demur; he sat at the back of the church, and when the service began his eyes strayed past the coffin in the centre of the aisle to the chief mourners seated to the right of it.

Aunt Matty was sitting alone, dressed in black. She was sitting very upright, as he knew she would.

There was no way in which she could have known he had entered the church and yet, in some indefinable manner, he felt she was aware of his presence and was resisting the impulse to turn her head. Alan was barely aware of the service itself, and he took no part in the responses. He stared at the back of his aunt's head and tried to subdue all the memories that flooded in on him, but then the service was over, and the pall-bearers were lifting the coffin, staggering slightly, and as the congregation left the church there was just the one moment when

Aunt Matty's eyes, behind the veil, flickered a cold, contemptuous glance of recognition at him.

Then he was alone in a silent church.

He waited, not quite understanding why he remained there, except perhaps from a vague sense of defiance. Jeff had been his brother; he had a right to be here; he had an obligation to be here. Yet he was unwilling to face those curious faces, so many unknown faces, outside. They would be getting into the black hired cars now for the one-mile drive to the cemetery. No place would have been allocated in any of the cars for Jeff Fearnley's brother.

But that was his own doing.

In a little while he rose, and walked out of the church. The sun had dimmed, and the narrow road outside the church was empty. The cars had gone, the congregation dispersed. The funeral procession of black cars would have driven down the road, turned right through the village and would now be taking the road up under the hill to the cemetery gates.

There was a shorter route on foot; Alan took it now, cutting behind the terraced houses above the church and following the footpath across the stream until he descended to the road outside the cemetery gates.

The cars were drawn up in a black line along the narrow roadway above him. The cluster of men — there were thirty or more — stood dark-suited in the sunshine, beside the open grave and outlined against the skyline while the priest muttered in the silent air. Alan walked slowly towards them, skirting the group and finally standing a little distance apart from them. There was someone else who appeared not to regard himself as part of this group: a small man with a narrow face, hands locked behind his back, round-shouldered in his stance but oddly watchful. He stood some thirty yards away and he stared at Alan for a few moments, as though curious about his presence. Then he turned away again, to watch the graveside group. None of them paid any attention to him, nor to Alan.

For a while Alan was able to recognize none of them, but gradually the odd movement of a head, the shuffling of feet, allowed him to stir chords of memory and he was able to link middle-aged bodies to younger, remembered faces. Even so, he knew very few of the exclusively male graveside congregation. Friends and acquaintances of his brother, the brother he had not seen for fifteen years, they were unknown to him.

Jeff Fearnley had carved out his own life; his own excitements; his own friendships. Alan Fearnley's had been far distant from this valley, in time and space and style. He watched the men leave, one by one, when the graveside service was concluded; some of them went quickly as though embarrassed at not knowing how to behave on such an occasion, while others lingered, perhaps equally embarrassed, making a brief show of taking their last farewells of the man who lay in the open grave. The cars quitted the scene, one by one, to make their way back to Aunt Matty's house, where she and the other women would be waiting, and at last there were only the two workmen at the graveside.

Alan looked across to where the other stranger had been standing. He was no longer there, but walking slowly down the hill, alone. As Alan watched him he glanced back, and hesitated, as though he was considering returning to speak to Alan, but then he turned away again, walked down the hill. Alan watched him until he disappeared through the gates and then he walked down to the graveside.

The two workmen had started to throw earth into the open grave. One paused, as Alan came up, waited for Alan to speak, but when he said nothing he shrugged and went on stolidly with his work.

Only then did Alan decide he would visit Aunt Matty.

*

The village, ribboning along the valley floor, was quiet, and the terraces of houses that rose along the valley sides were like lined sentinels watching over the river. Alan drove along, heading up the valley to Aunt Matty's and when he came to the street it seemed shabbier than he remembered it — or perhaps that was because of the expensive-looking cars that were now parked along its length. There were a dozen or more of them, and only three were family saloons. The rest were big, expensive vehicles, not new, but gleaming in the sunshine. Above them and across the roadway, beyond the broken fence and the tired, dirty stream, was the public park where he and Jeff had played as children and over which loomed the mountain. He remembered it as always rain-shrouded, but today it was ponderous and sleepy in the sun.

Alan was forced to park beyond the bend in the road, near the chapel; he walked past the chapel he and Jeff had not been allowed to attend even though all the other local children had joined its club, because Aunt Matty was a Catholic. There was the pub just a short way below: its decrepit sign proclaimed the New Inn with a faded bravado but no conviction. Uncle Joe had been allowed there three times each week, Aunt Matty doling out the money carefully. Two pints of beer, to be drunk in halves, and home half an hour before stop tap. Alan shook his head, remembering the grey cheeks and sad eyes of the man who had helped look after him from the time he was eight. How long since he had died?

The front door was open.

The green paint was peeling, but the brass knocker gleamed as brightly as ever, and the front step was almost white from its sanding. The passageway beyond was cool and dim, the stairs softly carpeted as they had not been in the old days, the walls expensively decorated with heavy wallpaper: Jeff's doing, no doubt. When Alan had left they had still been covered by brown, varnished mock panelling, a relic of the war years.

The front parlour was to the right, empty. The living-room was at the end of the passageway, leading into the kitchen, and it was from there that the sound of voices came. Alan hesitated, then walked forward, opened the glass-panelled door and looked in, framed in the doorway.

The room was crowded. Burly men stood with glasses in their hands, talking, yarning, grinning, laughing. The room beyond was not as he remembered it: the kitchen had been extended into the back yard so that it now comprised a larger area, a dining-room, with a new kitchen built beyond. A table had been laid there and a number of men were sitting around the table, with their wives, talking animatedly, drinking, eating. He saw the slices of cold ham, the fowl, the piles of buttered sliced bread, and he knew that nothing had changed, never would change.

'Drink?' The man beside him was grinning. 'Got a drink, man?'

Alan allowed a tumbler to be pushed into his hand, held it as half a bottle of beer was poured into it, and then he stood there, his back against the wall, a stranger in the house in which he had spent twelve years of his adolescent life.

Then heads turned suddenly in the dining-room, twitching as though jerked by invisible strings. Someone was staring at him, a woman. Her lips framed his name, other heads turned, some faces blank with incomprehension, others churning with curiosity, and the silence that grew in the dining-room spread like ripples in a pond to mark the room in which he stood.

Aunt Matty emerged from the kitchen, wiping her hands on her apron and her eyes met his, as they had done in the church, but now he could clearly see their coldness, and as the silence reached out and enveloped him he turned, walked back into the passageway and entered the empty front room. He was there, alone, for almost ten minutes, before anyone came in to join him.

II

'Alan?'

She would have been to the hairdresser's early that morning, specially for the funeral, and he wondered whether they would have tinted her hair, but it seemed to be as full of the reddish-dark lights as ever. Her face was fuller, rounded more about the chin, and there were tiny lines at the corners of her eyes, but those eyes were just as deeply brown as he remembered and the warmth of her smile reached out to him over the years.

'Hello, Marilyn,' he said, managing a smile, and after a moment's hesitation she came forward to him. He held out a hand but she ignored it; she stood close to him for a second and then, as impulsive as she had ever been, she threw her arms about him and hugged him. Her body was softer, her figure fuller, but he remembered the touch of her and he held her away from him, trembling slightly. She smiled, the smile turned to a healthy grin and she squeezed his hands.

'You've not changed, Alan Fearnley, not in fifteen years have you changed — except to get handsomer than I remember.'

'The years have treated *you* well, my girl, and you'd have got that compliment without telling lies about me!'

She shook her head, laughing, still holding both his hands. 'It's good to see you — but what a surprise! Why didn't you say you were coming?'

'Would I have been welcome?'

The words were out before he could bite them back and they sobered her. She looked at him solemnly for a few moments. 'I think your aunt would have welcomed you back almost any time. At least, from what I heard, up until the time your uncle died, anyway. After that . . .'

'And I'm late coming back now too, aren't I?' Alan said bitterly. 'You know, I never saw Jeff, not once during these last fifteen years. I wrote several times, suggesting he come up to stay but he made excuses, and then he stopped replying.'

And then Alan Fearnley stopped writing. Because he had moved into a different world, a different society, and his younger brother would not have been part of that society. Or so it had been said.

'Now you *have* come back, you'll see some changes.'

Alan responded to the attempt to change the subject. 'Not in you — and not all that much in the valley, really. It's greener, now the pits have been closed these years. And it seems . . . smaller, but I suppose that's a feeling everyone has, going back. As for the house here, well, it's certainly changed —'

Marilyn nodded. 'Jeff did a lot for your aunt in the house. Added a kitchen and a dining-room; had a bathroom built upstairs, extended the back bedroom. But then, he was earning good money once he left the factory, and since he stayed on living here, he didn't have all that much to spend his money on.'

Alan nodded. He turned his head, looking around the room. 'I never knew about *this*, you know.'

'*Never knew?*'

She sounded incredulous, flabbergasted, but she didn't understand. The world in which Alan Fearnley had moved for the last ten years had been far different from his background. Once he qualified as an accountant he had moved to a large firm in Manchester; some commercial connections he had made through company accounts had brought him an early directorship and marriage to the chairman's daughter. Thereafter, it was Sale and the gin-and-tonic belt, a heady involvement in a take-over bid that had placed him eventually on the board of an even larger company, and then there had been the trips to America, West Germany, France. Busy, exhilarating, tiring—and eventually, perhaps, self-defeating. But in that time he had not looked back to the valley, and had not seen what was happening to the brother he had left behind him, fourteen years of age.

Now, in this front room of the terrace house he remembered so well, the evidence was all around him. In a glass case, on top of the cupboard facing the window, silver trophies gleamed. Ranged along the cupboard itself were mounted medals, inscribed salvers, a carved glass block of doubtful taste and vulgar artistry. Pennants dangled limply from the wall, and over the fireplace were three framed photographs.

He had hardly recognized the man in the photographs as his brother. The years had thickened Jeff, broadened him, and beer had given him a paunch that was emphasized by the bright, lightning-flashed sweater he wore in the centre photograph. His hair had thinned, so the flashlight made him appear prematurely bald but he looked happy, grinning broadly and triumphantly, with the two runners-up for some trophy or other forcing smiles beside him as he nestled a gleaming cup against his belly.

'No, I never knew about it. I've never been particularly interested in any sport and . . . In fact, it's only because his death was reported in the newspapers in Bristol that I knew he'd been killed. Funny, in a way, isn't it? You see a headline, away from the sports page, about a darts champion being killed in a car crash, and it's your brother's name.'

'It must have been a terrible shock,' Marilyn said quietly.

'It was, of course, but . . .' There was no way he could
yet describe it; the feelings were too tangled and confused. A sense of failure; a feeling of having lost one's
way; a need to re-create the past; a desire to shelve the
present for a while and hide one's face from the future. A
time for private tears maybe — and perhaps they were un-
manly tears of frustration, self-pity and indecision. The
thought came to him now that maybe he had even
welcomed the news in that it had dragged him away from
his own, looming problems. Horrified, confused, he
could not meet Marilyn's glance and he stared around
him at the signs of Jeff's success. 'He . . . he was pretty
good, then.'

'He was the best.'

Alan turned, startled, at the sound of the man's voice.
He was standing in the doorway, a half glass of beer in his
hands. He was a short, deep-chested man in his mid-
forties, perhaps a little younger than Alan, but with grey
wings in his thick, curly hair. Carefully dressed, in a dark
grey suit and matching tie, he leaned against the door
jamb, staring at Alan curiously but obviously at home in
this house. Beside Alan, Marilyn stirred edgily.

'Alan, this is my husband, Jim Carter. Jim . . . this
is . . . this is Jeff's brother, Alan.'

Carter had thick, sensuous lips; they moved now,
wreathing into a smile warm in its welcome. He came
forward, extending a hand. 'Alan Fearnley! We've never
met . . . but I've heard about you.'

Again Marilyn stirred, and as Alan shook hands with
her husband he wondered from whom Jim Carter had
heard about the vanished big brother. In some matters,
he would have been able to learn more from Marilyn than
from Jeff Fearnley. But perhaps he already knew, Alan
thought, as he felt the competitive strength in the man's
grip.

'I thought I saw you up at the cemetery,' Carter was

saying. 'Wondered who you were at the time. Most of the others are from about here, you know. A stranger—'

'Alan's hardly a stranger,' Marilyn said, unable to keep the reproof out of her tone. Carter ignored her, but Alan was aware of the coldness with which he deigned to give her not even a glance.

'Not that I suppose you'd know many of them now around here,' Carter continued. 'The men at the church and up at the cemetery, a lot of them local, but some come from over the top, the other valleys, you know. One lad's from Merthyr, where I came from some years back to get married. Stayed afterwards, I did. Oh yes, they've come, as a mark of respect to Jeff.'

Alan thought of the big, flamboyant vehicles in the street outside. 'They . . . er . . . they'll be friends from the darts world?'

'Lot of them,' Carter nodded. 'Lot of them. And you never saw him play . . . Ha, man, you really missed something. He was the best . . . and given time, he'd have proved it. I tell you, when he used to come up to the oche—'

'Oche?'

Carter stared. 'Yeah, you know, the oche . . . the line behind which the thrower has to stand when he aims his arrows. Some of them have got buzzers installed these days, so if you step on it the foul throw is recorded. Anyway, as I was sayin', when he used to move up to the oche to throw he used to quiet the house. He'd grown into a big lad—the beer did that, because he needed to psyche himself up for the big ones with a few pints of lager—but he had a throwing action as delicate as eggshells. There was a kind of exploration with his wrist, like he was feeling the air, and then he just used to push that dart, smooth as steel on ice, in a perfect parabola. Spotlights, cameras, chanting crowds, none of it ever affected the smoothness of that movement—perfection. Talent and temperament, he had them both.' His deep-set eyes moved away from Alan to the photographs above the mantelpiece, and for a few seconds he seemed lost in thought. Then he shook his head. 'Ah, what a waste. Damn—what a waste!'

'You knew Jeff well?'

Jim Carter looked towards his wife in surprise, then turned back to Alan. 'We were close friends, weren't we? We worked the clubs for years, and it was I who persuaded him to leave the factory, concentrate on the arrows, because with his skill there was money to be made. I trained him, made him sweat at it, protected him—aye, I knew him well. And I had plans . . . He was to be the king pin, best in my stable—'

'You became his business manager?'

Carter grimaced, nodded. 'That's about the size of it. Never had a written contract, of course, because we didn't need one. We trusted each other, understood each other. And he needed . . . guidance.' Jim Carter hesitated, eyeing Alan carefully for a moment. 'You hadn't seen him in years?'

'That's right.'

Carter gave a quiet, almost affectionate snort. 'He hadn't changed much, if at all. He must have been soft as muck when he was a kid, and he was the same when he was sixteen stone. Anyone could twist him—open-handed, and always ready to be ruled.' Again he looked at Alan Fearnley. 'It's why he never left this house, of course.'

Alan could guess what he meant. Aunt Matty had always had a strong personality, a domineering manner and mind. She would not have wanted Jeff to leave the house, so he would have stayed.

'He could have afforded a damn sight better,' Carter was saying thoughtfully. 'You know, just before he turned pro he was picking up just forty quid a week, and that was

with overtime. We'd teamed up in the local New Inn
darts club and there wasn't a lad in the valley could hold
him. I saw the way the wind was blowing, and when the
money started pumping into the game—you know, once
TV got hold of it, the whole thing took off—I knew
he could make the big time. But I had one hell of a job
persuading him to jack in his job in the factory. And he
ended up making a hundred a week—just for throwing
darts. And he could have made more, but he just
wouldn't allow himself to be used in advertising.'

'I imagine Aunt Matty wouldn't have wanted him . . .
er . . . showing off,' Alan said drily.

Carter glanced at him quizzically, then chuckled.
'That's right. Still, he was making enough. The first year
we worked the clubs and I arranged the side betting; the
second year it wasn't necessary: the appearance money
and the prizes he won meant the job was easy. He was
headed right to the top—and when I pulled his main rival
into the team, we had a really sweet group going.'

'Rival?'

'Freddy Thomas. Beautiful player. Didn't have Jeff's
appeal—you know, big Teddy Bear Jeff as opposed to
quiet concentration and commitment—and didn't have
his talent either. But the three of us, hell, we were coining
it.'

'You'll miss him, all right,' Marilyn said.

Carter glanced at her sharply. There had been no edge
in the remark that Alan could have detected, but a
married couple had their own razors that were often im-
perceptible to outsiders. Alan Fearnley knew all about
that. And maybe, in some way, Marilyn had just scored
Carter's nerves.

'So what'll you do now?' Alan asked.

Carter turned back to him, shrugging. 'Press on.
There's the first legs of the Nationals coming up: Jeff
would have walked them, and would have won through

without a doubt at the end. He worked well with Freddy,
you see: the two of them, they sort of had their own little
needle going whenever they were in competition. Jeff
recognized that, realized Freddy pushed him. That was
why we had the financial arrangement we did.'

'What was that?'

'We pooled everything. Winnings and expenses.' He
smiled deprecatingly. 'I usually entered myself, at the
beginning. Later on, I stepped back, organized things
behind the scenes, let them two slug it out. I kept things
smooth for them, and they came in with the winnings. It
was a good system. Aye, like Marilyn says, I'll miss him all
right.'

'And Freddy Thomas?'

Jim Carter's eyes were cool and appraising. He
scratched his cheek thoughtfully. 'Ah well, you got to
remember, Freddy always did have aspirations. He never
really believed Jeff was better than him — even though the
occasions he beat your brother were few and far between.
The gap was widening, in fact, but Freddy'd never accept
that. And, well, there are times when he's so . . . committed, it's frightening. So, though he and Jeff were pals
enough, I reckon almost the first thing Freddy would've
thought, when he heard Jeff . . . was dead, it would have
been that the National was in his grasp now, with the big
one gone. But that's human, isn't it?'

Or inhuman, Alan thought. 'Was he at the funeral
today?'

Carter glanced at Marilyn. She shook her head. 'He
rang up last night. Said he couldn't make it.'

'He'll be limbering up, somewhere,' Carter said. 'Cold
bastard, really, whichever way you look at it.' He finished
his beer. 'You like another drink, Alan?'

'No, thanks, I've still got some left.'

'I'll go stock up. Be back in a second. Marilyn?'

She shook her head, and watched her husband leave

the room. There was a short, awkward silence. Alan cleared his throat. 'How long you been married?'

She raised her eyebrows, and shrugged. 'Eight years, just about.'

'Seems a nice chap.' The triteness of the remark seemed to cause a degree of tension to arise between them, and Alan turned to inspect the photographs again. The third one had signatures scrawled on it—four men with their arms around each other's shoulders, Jeff to the left. It had been taken in a club of some kind; a trophy lay at Jeff's feet. Alan leaned forward to read the scrawled signatures. One of them was more than a signature: '*You lucky bugger—Freddy.*'

'Which one is Freddy Thomas?' he asked.

'On the right. The slim one, with the dark hair.' Her tone held an edge of displeasure, an irritated, puzzled note as though she was faced with something she had thought long gone. 'You never wrote once, Alan.'

Perhaps he had half expected the accusation. He turned to face her. 'There didn't seem much point.'

. 'You could have written, to say how you were.'

'It . . . it was pointless. I wasn't coming back; I didn't come back. And you didn't want to leave the valley, while I *had* to, or suffocate.'

'But just a *note*, for God's sake, to say whether you were alive or dead!'

He stared at her, holding her glance steadily. He shook his head. 'It's all such a long time ago, love.'

She made no reply, and her glance slipped away from his. Someone was walking along the passageway into the house; the footsteps hesitated at the door and Marilyn turned, looked around the open door. 'Danny! You made it then!'

He came in, gave her a perfunctory peck on the cheek, and turned his pale face in Alan's direction. The sad, lugubrious expression looked as though it had been pasted on his face for the occasion, the insincerity of a showman projecting the image for the day, matching mood to surroundings. The eyes gave the expression away: they were sharp, penetrating needle points of curiosity. He was of middle height, expensively suited, with a regulation black armband and subdued tie. His face was lean, hollow-cheeked, his mouth thin-lipped, but used to creating a professional smile. His thinning hair was carefully parted low on one side of his head, to cover the bare temples and he raised one slim hand now, to smooth at a sideburn in an unconscious gesture born of nervousness. A man used to crowds, perhaps, but always wary of strangers.

'Aunt Matty in?' he asked Marilyn, slipping his glance from Alan for a moment. 'In the back, I mean.'

'It's pretty crowded back there—I should wait for a while before you offer your condolences. She'd prefer that—she hoped you'd have made it to the funeral.'

'No chance. Just got in from Stoke. Fixing the deal for the 20th. Er . . .'

His eyes were back to Alan again, and Marilyn apologized. 'I'm sorry, Danny—this is Jeff's brother Alan. Danny Elias. He . . . he promoted Jeff quite a lot.'

'Jeff's brother?' The narrow eyes widened, startled, and there was something else in them, deep down, a hint of swift calculation, a reckoning of odds. 'Never spoke about having a brother.'

'I've been away for fifteen years. We . . . we didn't really keep in touch.'

'Alan didn't even know Jeff was a champion at darts,' Marilyn explained.

'And *I* was telling him Jeff was about top of the heap,' the interruption came again, a repeat performance from Jim Carter. 'Hello, Danny, glad you could make it. Back from Stoke?'

'That's right. All fixed. The semi-finals will be held

there — the Aussie and that bastard from Scotland will be there. International night all right!' The quick burst of enthusiasm died suddenly, as though Elias recalled where he was. He looked back to Alan. 'And you didn't know that your brother would have been kingpin within the year! I'd have bet on it. In fact, I *did* bet on it. Even though that last night at Swansea . . .'

His eyelids flickered, a tremor of caution touching his eyes. Alan waited, but Elias said no more. Carter thrust his beer in his hand. 'Here, you have this one. I'll get another. Just hold on a bit.'

Elias nodded, glanced around the room, and sipped at his drink. 'You'll have been older than Jeff.'

'Six years.'

'And what's your line of country?'

'I'm an accountant. I work in the Midlands, mostly, but my company sent me down to Bristol to do a job at Avonmouth docks. That's where I was when I read about Jeff's death.'

'Sad. Sad business.' It might have been embarrassment that made Elias shy away from talk of Jeff's death, but he seemed disinclined to talk of it. 'Big firm you work for?'

'Pretty big. It includes a shipbuilding contract now, but mainly it's concerned with light engineering projects. The Avonmouth deal is a bit different, though . . .'

Danny Elias wasn't really interested, but he kept the conversation going, while Marilyn remained quietly in the background. Jim Carter came back, and after a little while the conversation edged away from Alan, and got nearer to their own interests. Their discussion of the relative merits of the more fancied players likely to reach the semi-finals at Stoke was almost incomprehensible to Alan, and certainly of no interest to him, but he stood woodenly beside them, aware that Marilyn was watching him silently, but refusing to meet her glance.

These men were strangers in the house in which he had

lived; the noise that came from the other rooms was the relaxing of tension after a funeral; he had no real idea what he was doing here again, when he had shaken the black dust of the valley from his shoes fifteen years ago; his brother was dead, his aunt awaited him in the other room, and he didn't want to be here.

And yet, at this point in time, he knew there was nowhere else he could go.

It left him particularly vulnerable, when they had all gone, and he finally faced Aunt Matty.

III

'Why have you come back?'

She stood there facing him when they had all gone, a tiny, dark-visaged hawk of a woman, spare to the point of emaciation but with eyes like claws, that could dig deep and rend, tear away fiction and deceit, rarely sheathed, even, he suspected, when she slept. As a boy, he had fancied that those eyes still glittered in the midnight darkness, full of the need to watch against the harshness of life — an existence in which she had seen her younger sister die at her second childbirth, leaving Matty with two young nephews to raise, after their father died in a pit accident, two years later. Saddled with a grey-faced, weak-kneed husband more eager to visit the New Inn than do a week's work in the pit, and with two boys to rule and mould, her life had lacked some satisfaction she craved, and it had sharpened her tongue, hardened her determination and her view of life. And now the old man was gone, and Jeff was gone, and the boy she had never held, never controlled, had returned.

He stood tongue-tied for a little while, and her eyes burned at him. 'You didn't come back for your uncle,' she accused him. 'So why now?'

'I . . . I didn't know Uncle Joe had died, until later.' Someone had sent him a cutting from the local newspaper. An anonymous well-wisher, wanting to turn a knife—your uncle dead, why weren't you there? 'And then I felt—'

'He thought a lot of you,' Aunt Matty cut in. 'Used to talk about you, up in the pub. Not in here. I wouldn't have him talk about you in here. Not after the way you treated us; not after the way you showed us how little gratitude you felt for me and him. And how little you thought of your own brother, too.'

Alan Fearnley felt the years ebbing away; he was no longer a grown man. His aunt could do that to him— make him feel hesitant, fearful. He shook his head. 'I wrote to Jeff several times, asking him to come stay with me. After I got married—'

'He didn't want to come,' she said sharply. 'He showed me the letters; we talked about it. His home was here, and there was no call to go traipsing around the country, just because you called him, to follow in your footsteps. He was *proud* to stay back here with us, and he got a good job—'

'In a factory!' Alan snapped at her. 'For God's sake, Aunt Matty, if he'd have come to join me I could have helped set him up in the firm I was with, and he could have made something of himself! Working in a factory!'

Her hands trembled; the veins stood out on the backs of those hands, thick, heavy snakes marking blue tracks under her skin. 'There was nothing wrong with working in a factory! It was honest work. And he *did* make something of himself. And maybe that's why you're back, is it? It's the money, is it?' She glared at him triumphantly. 'Well, I can tell you, he made a will, and you're not mentioned in it at all!'

He stared at her, and felt the confusion of emotions

that were tangled in her brain — anger, a sense of loss that she would find difficult to express, and the malice of her words struck him forcibly. His mouth was dry. 'The money he had is of no importance to me. I came back to see him buried, that's all.'

Her eyes were unnaturally bright. She seemed not to have heard him. 'I knew you'd come back one day. I knew you'd come back with honeyed words, try to take him away, leave me the way you left me. But he would never have done it; he was *my* boy.'

'He was nearly thirty, Aunt Matty,' Alan said gently.

'And when he made all that money I was determined he wouldn't waste it. I banked it for him, every time he won. And I told him to make a will so you wouldn't get your hands on it, when he died. And he loved me so much he left it to me, because he was grateful, and he knew what he owed me . . .'

Her hands were trembling again, more violently now, and some of the fierce passions died in her eyes. Alan reached out and touched her shoulder; she flinched, but then relaxed as he slipped his arm about her. 'Come in the kitchen,' he said gently. 'I'll make you a cup of tea.'

He needed time to consider what crawled in her mind through a tangled hedge of pain and loss and hurt. He had always known she would never show forgiveness for what she saw as desertion; he had known he would never be able to explain to her how suffocated he was by her fierce control of their lives and their minds. He had felt it necessary to leave her and the valley, to breathe. It had been as basic a need as that. But she would never understand.

And her inability to understand had grown like a canker in her mind until the possessive love she had felt for him and Jeff had in his case turned to something near hate — and in Jeff's case to a complete domination. Jeff would have complied for the sake of peace, even to the extent of making a will to please her, giving everything to her after his death, in spite of the fact that she was now gone sixty years of age. And it had been because of Alan's leaving, fifteen years ago.

The tea warmed her, calmed her and she brushed her thinning hair back from her eyes with patting gestures as she studied him less directly now, sitting opposite her. She was looking for signs of weakness, in his mouth and eyes; signs of carelessness in his dress; intimations of anxiety in his bearing, anything that might give her an opening to attack, and wound. He met her glance, flickering over him, calmly.

'Do you really hate me that much, Aunt Matty?'

He had never before seen alarm in her eyes, but it flashed there, then retreated, like a cat before a dog. Her head came up, the chin pointing at him, and behind a mask of confident surprise, she said, 'Hate you, boy? Don't be ridiculous! You've not been important enough to me for these last fifteen years, to *hate*.' She made a humphing noise and looked down at the tablecloth, making tiny sweeping movements with her hand, as though removing memories with the scattered crumbs. 'You don't hate someone you've dismissed from your mind. You were always a source of unhappiness to me. When you left the Church, that was one thing. I prayed for you then, and I talked to the Father, but your self-will was too strong, too determined. So determined I guessed then it wasn't because you lacked faith: you wanted to cross *me*.'

He did not believe that was true, but if he were to say he had left because he did not believe, it would do nothing to help him in her eyes. 'It's a long time ago, Aunt Matty.'

She appeared not to have heard him. 'And when you wrote, afterwards, to Jeff, it was to try to take him away from us. Not because you wanted him, or cared enough to help him get on, as you say now. It was to strike at me. Ingratitude . . .'

There was simply no point in arguing with her. Learning of Jeff's death had been a great shock to him, and he had come back for the funeral. But it had been a mistake to see Aunt Matty again. It helped neither of them. She was filled with the memories of past wrongs—his desertion of her Church and her home; his attempts to win from her the young boy she still dominated; his failure to return when Uncle Joe had died, even though there was no way he could have known of the old man's illness.

'But I've wondered,' she continued with a spark of malice, 'whether it was *all* your doing. When you said you were getting married I could guess how it would all be. I knew she would be too hoity-toity for the likes of us. I knew that the kind of Englishwoman you'd marry, with your big ideas, and your ambition, would be the kind who'd look down on us who'd brought you up, given you everything we could. I knew she'd never visit us, never come to the valley with you. Not that you'd have brought her, I suppose, because you'd have moved on, and up, and you wouldn't want to be reminded of it all, of the place where you'd come from. Bit of both, was it? Two of a kind?' Perhaps there was something unspoken in his eyes; more likely, she guessed because of that strange capacity she had always had, to look almost into his soul and read what lay there. 'Not with you now, is she? What is it—trouble, then? Things not the way they were, or were supposed to be? Is *that* why you came back?'

Stiffly Alan said, 'I told you why I came back. Jeff—'

'Was your brother, and twice the man you'll ever be, and all you've ever done for him is to come back and help bury him.' She began to cry, but they were soundless tears and Alan had no real knowledge of what had prompted them. It could have been the loss of her favourite nephew; but, he suspected, it might be something else, connected with him. He would probably never know.

'I'll be going soon,' he said, glancing at his watch. 'If I'm to get back to Bristol—'

'You're not staying?' she asked sharply, and brushed away the tears with the back of her thin hand.

'I didn't think you'd—'

'There's so much to do,' she said in a fierce tone, 'and I've no one with any sense to help me. I would never have asked you to come back, but you *have*, so the least you can do is help me get things sorted out.'

'I've not booked a room anywhere and—'

'There's no need. Jeff's room is tidy—I rooted everything out before the funeral. Or if you don't like the idea of his room, there's the one in the back you used to use when you lived here. I can soon get the bed aired.'

She hadn't changed, and neither had he. Already it was as though Jeff's death was relegated to the back of her mind, dismissed now that he had left her, for good: Alan was back, and had to be organized, tied down, *crippled* in will and self-determination. He felt the pulse in his forehead beat in unreasoning anger, and he shook his head. 'I'm sorry, Aunt, there are things I must do in the office. I must get back.'

'I *need* you, Alan,' she said after a short silence. It was a word he had never heard her use before. Need. He understood that word in certain contexts, and understood its lack of fulfilment. He himself had his own other, indefinable need, that in some way had something to do with this house and the valley, and to some degree that was why he was back now, not just to bury his brother but to answer other questions in his mind. But Aunt Matty had always been too self-centred, too controlled to feel need—or at least to admit it. Till now. Alan stared at her for a little while and the greyness of her skin was gradually tinged with colour, a faint flush, as though she was embarrassed at what she had just said to him. Then her breast heaved as she took a deep breath. Her voice was calm as she spoke. 'I'm an old woman, Alan, and I never wanted you back. I wrote you out of my life the day you left us. But I *am* old and I'm alone and . . . there are things I don't understand. You've had education; you're a professional man. You can help me. Jeff made a lot of money. He put some in the bank, some in building societies, some in this house. And there's his will. I don't know what to do about things and I've never trusted solicitors.'

'There'll be executors named in the will,' Alan demurred. 'Any legal firm —'

'I want *you* to look into it, do what needs to be done. No need to pay good money to crooked lawyers. Besides, you *owe* it to me. You're here, you're back, and I think you're under an *obligation* to help me after the way you've behaved.'

He could not meet the determined glitter in her eyes. He poured himself another cup of tea, nodding. 'I'll stay tonight, Aunt Matty, but I *will* have to go back to Bristol in the morning.' She opened her mouth to protest but he forestalled her. 'It'll take me best part of the day to sort things out but then I'll come back. And I'll see what needs to be done to get probate of the will.'

'It's the least you can do,' she said unforgivingly.

He made no reply.

After all, it shouldn't take too long, and it would give him a little more time, perhaps, to delay the decisions that faced him in Bristol.

CHAPTER 2

I

Alan left the house early next morning without seeing his aunt. He drove swiftly through the quiet streets of the valley, out on the Cardiff road and then east towards Newport and the Severn Bridge.

By nine o'clock he was at his desk in the Bristol office of Emburey Associates, and Sally, the pert-nosed secretary, was bringing him a cup of coffee. There was a neat stack of papers on his desk, the way he had left them before he drove to the valley, and he was reluctant to look at them again, knowing what they contained. He sipped his coffee, swivelled in his chair and stared out of the window across the Bristol skyline.

He wondered what Diana was doing.

She would know what he should do about the papers on his desk. His wife always had a very positive view about everything, particularly when it was connected with business. Maybe that was why he had married her in the first instance: she had seemed so *definite* about everything, including wanting Alan Fearnley. That, and perhaps the fact that he had not escaped the effects of Aunt Matty's domination completely, had led him into his own early decision to ask Diana to marry him.

And he had done well since. Diana had been a great help. The contacts her father had made for him, and later, those she had personally fostered, they had all meant for him a swift, successful rise in the accountancy world, and early transition to board of director status. Oh yes, Diana had been a great help. She had seen it as her role, to help him get on.

In any way she deemed necessary.

Savagely he swivelled back in his chair and glared at the papers on his desk. He checked his desk diary. Stevenson would be coming to see him at ten o'clock. It would be as well to prepare again, carefully, for the interview. The solicitor would have some searching questions to ask, and it was necessary that Alan have the right kind of answers.

Stevenson arrived precisely at ten. He was a lawyer of the old school: perhaps sixty years of age, he was dressed in a dark, pin-striped suit and white-collared, blue-and-white-striped shirt. His hair was neatly parted and pasted down, every hair in place; his eyes were a young, piercing blue; his mouth thin-lipped, inclined to purse thoughtfully; his manner exact, precise, and disconcertingly sharp. Politeness was nevertheless his most polished asset; it could conceal a razor tongue, as Alan had once seen demonstrated in the courtroom, and it could also persuade a man to dismiss Stevenson as an old-world fool, but Alan knew the solicitor to be perceptive—and dangerous.

Now, he was extending his hand, smiling, expressing delight to be meeting Alan Fearnley again. Yes, he would love to have a cup of coffee; no, he did not smoke, for he had an unreasonable desire to cling to life as long as he could. Polite remarks about the weather, the city, and enquiries after the health of Alan's wife followed, and only when the coffee had been brought in by Sally did Stevenson finally sigh, reach for his pen, and open a small notebook which he placed on the desk in front of him.

'Well, Mr Fearnley, I suppose we'd better get down to the reason for my visit. You won't object if I take a few notes of our discussions this morning? At my age, memory can play tricks, and I always think it's better to have an agreed note of conversations. That way, ah . . . disputes about what was actually said or determined can be avoided, don't you agree?'

Alan agreed, but looked at the notebook with a jaundiced eye, nevertheless. He knew perfectly well that it could at some time provide a most useful piece of evidence, if the solicitor ever decided to use it.

'I'll come straight to the point, Mr Fearnley. You will perhaps already be aware that I am representing a group of businessmen from . . . ah . . . Spain and Switzerland, all of whom are in the hotel and catering business?'

'So I understand.'

'You will also be aware that they are, shall we say, concerned about the present financial state of one of their major clients, Sunski Ltd, of London, a firm with which, I believe, Emburey Associates has some connection?'

Alan nodded. 'We act as their auditors, yes.'

'Auditors . . .' Stevenson flicked an invisible piece of fluff from his pin-striped trouser leg as he pondered on the word. 'Yes . . . well, to continue. My instructions are to carry out certain . . . ah . . . enquiries into the financial status of Sunski as a result of certain actions that have been taken recently.' He flicked back a few pages in his notebook and consulted some figures. 'We needn't go into the details of trading figures over the last year or so, but suffice it to say that the group of hoteliers for whom I act lay claim to a fairly large sum of money, due to them from Sunski. You do regard £100,000 as a fairly large sum, Mr Fearnley?'

'Certainly.' Alan hesitated. 'I believe that is the total liability, but from the records I understood quite a large part of that sum has been the subject of payments made during the last month.'

'Ah yes.' Stevenson almost purred with pleasure. 'But that's the reason for my visit this morning, in fact. My clients inform me that the cheques made over were drawn upon an organization called . . . ah . . . Continentalbank Incorporated.'

'I believe that's right.'

Stevenson smiled thinly. 'The cheques have been dishonoured, Mr Fearnley.'

Alan made no reply, and the silence grew around them. Stevenson reached forward and sipped at his coffee; he was in no hurry to press issues, but equally, Alan was not prepared to rush into any damaging statements. He first had to discover what Stevenson knew, before he made up his own mind about what he should do.

'Your silence,' Stevenson said at last, 'tells me nothing of the state of your own knowledge of the dealings of Sunski and Continentalbank Inc. Most properly, of course, as an auditor appointed by Sunski you will wish to keep to yourself information that has come to you in a professional capacity, but there are occasions when the retention of certain information can be, shall we say, dangerous to the holder?' He smiled again, coldly. 'But no more of that for the moment. Perhaps I should tell you the result of my own enquiries, which now brings me to you. At my clients' request, I have carried out certain investigations into the activities of Sunski Ltd, and its history. The company began operations, I understand, in 1972?'

'That is correct.'

'The entrepreneur—or, I should perhaps say, *entrepreneuse?*—was a lady called Ella Shore who showed considerable flair in establishing what she called a sun-and-snow holiday firm, undercutting other organizations by using small and unfashionable resorts in Spain and Switzerland, but attractive and out-of-the-way places nevertheless. In 1975, when expansion became necessary, the firm took in new directors and obtained funding from new external sources.'

'I have a list of the directors,' Alan offered. 'They include some substantial—'

'But no doubt sleeping, executives,' Stevenson interrupted, failing by the coldness of his smile to remove the bite from the remark. 'Yes . . . Now as far as I can see, Sunski might have begun to overreach itself when it purchased Villa Franchises Ltd, in 1977.'

'I think that must be a matter of opinion, Mr Stevenson.'

'To which each of us are individually entitled, Mr Fearnley. The facts, as opposed to opinions, are that Sunski *did* buy Villa Franchises, that the purchase gave them certain visible assets, but that their profit margins fell considerably during the course of the year as the result of certain difficulties over non-existent, or unfinished, hotels in Spain.'

'Not entirely their fault, I think.'

'And I concede,' murmured the solicitor. 'But at the same time, linking with Villa Franchises, Sunski attempted to promote a certain resort in Spain—with a certain lack of success, would you not agree?'

'The figures—'

'So disclose, I would argue,' Stevenson interrupted emphatically, 'but you need make no comment on that, Mr Fearnley. Nor need you comment upon, or confirm, the other fact in my possession. In 1978 the International Air Transport Association withdrew from Sunski all airline ticket facilities. This action, I understand, was taken after they had checked the company balance sheet. Which your firm had prepared.'

'*Audited*, Mr Stevenson.'

The solicitor conceded the point with a deprecatingly raised hand. He consulted his notebook again. 'Thereafter, there was what may be described as a management reshuffle, some new directors again—with the more illustrious names withdrawing, though again I ask for no comment, Mr Fearnley — and then we come to the crucial time, as far as I can see. IATA facilities were restored, as a result of the improved financial situation of Sunski.'

Alan inclined his head in assent. Stevenson's eyes were suddenly watchful. 'Would you care to tell me what kind of rescue operation was carried out?' the solicitor asked. 'To begin with, what was the size of indebtedness at that time?'

'It's a matter of public record,' Alan said diffidently. 'You may well have seen an article in one of the Sunday newspapers—'

'Ah yes, there was a newspaper investigation, I recall.'

'The article,' Alan said in a firm voice, 'was not accurate in many of its statements, and some of its comments came close to being libellous, but they were accurate in the amount of money owed. It was in the region of £250,000.'

Stevenson nodded his narrow head. 'I think that's right. But then, early in 1979, all was well again. Would you be prepared to comment?'

Alan hesitated. He had no idea how much Stevenson really knew, and how deeply he was fishing. 'I think,' he said slowly, 'I can make the following statements without destroying any of my clients's confidence. Sunski were in debt to the tune of a quarter of a million, but they had sound assets — true, they were unrealizable at their proper value, but there was the basis of a sound business there — and they took their case to . . . to an American company. That company was prepared to extend them a line of credit to the extent of £200,000. Sunski began to draw on that credit in 1979, and also began to pay into the credit organization concerned certain rather smaller sums, as they were received. A perfectly normal business operation.'

'Quite so. But the cheques have recently been dishonoured,' Stevenson said. When Alan made no reply, he

went on, 'I hope you are able to confirm that the line of
credit was extended to Sunski by Continentalbank Inc.?'

After a moment's hesitation, Alan nodded. 'That is so.'

'And the American company which arranged the
credit — would that be Fernline International?'

Alan looked at the papers on his desk. Stevenson had
been doing his homework well; he knew more than Alan
suspected. Reluctantly he nodded again. 'Representations
were made to Fernline International in 1978. It was that
company that arranged the line of credit.'

'Who *are* Fernline International, Mr Fearnley?'

The solicitor's tone was soft, but there was steel
beneath the velvet. Alan met his glance, but without
much confidence. 'I've no doubt you'll find it easy enough
to check on their directorate and their activities.'

Stevenson held his narrow head to one side, glancing at
Alan quizzically. 'Ah well, that is a moot point. There are
ways in which a determined man can avoid disclosure of
his activities . . . and interlocking directorates are
sometimes difficult to determine. So I will ask you
another question. Who are Continentalbank Inc.?'

'Once again — ' Alan began.

'Once again, your answer will no doubt be unhelpful.
However, as an auditor of Sunski accounts you will
naturally be able to help by providing me with relevant
papers, in due course . . .' He paused, eyeing Alan carefully. 'It may be, of course, that my clients will never get
the answers they feel they deserve; equally, it may be that
my own efforts will be doomed to failure. But I have a
feeling about this whole situation, Mr Fearnley, and I
simply do not know whether it is shared by you. My visit
today was merely to ask a few opening questions: there
will be others, if my researches prove fruitful. But I would
like to put one fact to you. A *professional* fact, for we are
both professional men. An auditor has certain professional duties, does he not?'

'He does.'

'I believe the general statement is that he is to be regarded as a watchdog, rather than a bloodhound, but I've always felt that understates his duties.'

'Which lie to the company which employs him.'

'Quite so,' Stevenson agreed, and eyed Alan carefully. 'But not entirely, of course. He must be honest . . . that is to say, he must not certify what he does not believe to be true, and he must exercise reasonable care and skill before he considers that what he certifies is true.'

'I do believe,' Alan said mockingly, 'that you've been looking up your authorities.'

'I need look up no authority,' Stevenson replied in a frosty tone, 'for the proposition, which is of a general nature, that an auditor must not be negligent — and that is a duty he owes to anyone who might be induced, as a result of his statements, to deal with or invest in the company in question.'

'I am fully conversant with that duty,' Alan said, his own voice turning cold. 'But I don't see —'

'And I need hardly add the question of criminal liability, which arises under a number of Acts starting with the Larceny Act of 1861, the Falsification of Accounts Act 1875 and proceeding through to —'

'Mr Stevenson,' Alan cut in, 'I don't think I really require a lesson in the law relating to auditors. Nor do I entirely see just what you're getting at.'

Stevenson injected mild surprise into his voice and eyes; the attempt was only fairly successful. 'I was merely pointing out that I sympathize with the difficulties you have to face in your task as an auditor. It is so easy to make a slip in such matters — the presentation of accounts and background information on a company can so easily mislead. But I am certain you are far too experienced to fall into such errors. I've no doubt your audited statements regarding Sunski are, and will be, quite in order.'

'I don't believe my professional competence or integrity
has ever been called into question,' Alan said stiffly.

'Quite so, quite so. And you will presently be working
on Sunski accounts, so I really shouldn't take up more of
your time. You'll have plenty to do.' Stevenson rose to his
feet. 'Thank you for your coffee. No, don't get up — I'm
sure I can find my own way out.' He turned, walked
towards the door and then paused, as though struck by a
sudden thought. 'Ah, there is one more thing. The
woman who founded Sunski . . . didn't she have some
connection with Emburey Associates?'

'Ella Shore?' Alan nodded. 'That's right. She was married to Peter Emburey.'

'Was?'

'They were divorced some years ago.'

'But maintained their connection, so to speak,' the
solicitor said, with a smile. 'Through your firm, I mean.
Emburey Associates, acting as auditors to Sunski. It's nice
to be reassured that the pain of a divorce does nothing to
damage a business relationship. I'll say good day now, Mr
Fearnley.' He bobbed his head and walked to the door.
'I'm sure we'll meet again.'

Alan was certain he would have loved to add — *in court*.

He pondered over the visit, and the conversation, for the
rest of the morning. The parting shot about Ella Shore
was quite deliberately included: it was designed to show
Alan Fearnley that Stevenson knew a great deal about the
background to Sunski and Continentalbank. Similarly,
the little discourse had been meant as a warning, when he
had talked about the duties of an auditor. He was stress-
ing that with his hotelier clients in the background, he
would certainly be running a fine-tooth comb over the
audited accounts — and the slightest discrepancy would be
pounced upon, perhaps to Alan Fearnley's discomfiture.

Or maybe there was more to it than that. Maybe he

already had some idea what lay in the files in front of Alan Fearnley right now. Stevenson would know that part of the auditor's duty would be the certification, at least by implication, of certain transactions accepted in the audit. That certification could be important to outsiders—they would rely upon the auditor's statement.

But how far was an auditor under a duty to check? *A watchdog, not a bloodhound* . . . but if his suspicions were aroused, what then?

He stared at the files in front of him. The papers in that stack raised certain questions, awkward questions that could not in all professional conscience be side-stepped. But what if the answers that emerged were what he feared they might be? At the moment, all he held were certain vague suspicions. The problem would really bite if those suspicions were translated into certainties.

He opened the files and looked again at his notes. The queries, and the steps necessary to answer them, were all there, pencilled in his usual precise hand. Precision. Perhaps he was being *too* precise. Perhaps he should shrug off the suspicions, in spite of the veiled hints that the solicitor Stevenson had uttered. But essentially, Alan Fearnley knew he was unable to do that; quite apart from Stevenson's attitude, the auditor had to ask the questions—whatever it might cost, and even if there could be other, deeper, more personal motives behind asking questions in the first place. Alan Fearnley was no longer able to divorce personal from professional matters and the confusion bothered him, caused him to delay, uncertainly.

Yet the job had to be done—now, or later. It was what was to come afterwards that provided the real problem. Reluctantly, he picked up the phone.

II

The following morning Alan walked across the park that lay opposite Aunt Matty's house and climbed the hill beyond.

The track he followed was an old, familiar one. It wandered around the shoulder of the hill until the terraces below were lost to view and then crossed the ancient tramline that had been used to transport coal from the level driven into the hillside a hundred years ago. The pit workings had long since fallen into decay, but when Alan crossed the stream with its wooded banks and reached the old level it was as though he were a child again, with Jeff, playing among the ruined walls of the winding house, scrambling over the rusted boilers, their voices echoing from the hillside in the long summer afternoons.

Now it was quiet, and it held not only memories for him but a prospect of peace for a little while, avoiding the problems that beset him. He sat down on the boulders that were strewn beside the stream and watched the meagre water rush past his feet. Aunt Matty was sitting in the house down below, and there would be visitors calling to talk to her; later this morning Alan would need to go through what papers Jeff had left, checking bank statements and deposit books, but for now he just wanted to clear his mind. Here, with the sound of the dashing water, and the warm sunshine on his back, he might find the opportunity to escape for a little while.

Minutes later, the stone splashing into the water in front of him brought him back to reality. Startled, he turned to look behind him. Marilyn was standing there, some ten yards away, grinning at him. She was dressed in corded jeans that emphasized her hips and legs; the short-sleeved yellow shirt was left carelessly unbuttoned at the throat and her skin was tanned to the swell of her breast. He scrambled to his feet, facing her.

'I thought you might come up here,' she said. 'I was on my way up to Aunt Matty's — she told me you'd be coming back last night — and then I saw you walking along the track. So, shameless as I am, I followed you. Can two sit down and dream?'

Alan smiled. 'Be my guest.' She walked forward and perched herself on one of the large boulders; Alan sat down again, a little below her and a short distance away. She looked at him critically.

'I was up there for about ten minutes, watching you. You seemed preoccupied.'

He nodded. 'Just avoiding thinking, really, but it's not easy, even here.'

'Jeff?'

'In part. We used to come here as kids; it was a good place. I thought I'd be able to get a few things out of my system. But it doesn't really work.'

Marilyn frowned, and stared down at the water. 'I hope you won't mind me saying so, Alan, but you can't really be missing Jeff. I mean, you didn't really keep in touch.'

He shrugged. 'That's right . . . but coming back here . . .'

'Jeff should have done the same as you,' she said. 'You were right to get out; you've done well. But I think he was simply never able to screw up the courage or determination to break away from Aunt Matty. It wasn't that she wasn't good to him: she looked after him well, gave him all the creature comforts, and though she used to play up a bit when he got home really late, of recent years even that changed. She realized he had to be with girls, some-times . . .'

Alan smiled ruefully. 'She's changed, then. She made it damned difficult for me to take any girl in the village out.'

'You managed, though,' Marilyn said quietly, and he glanced sharply at her. For a moment she still stared at the stream, and then her eyes met his and it was as though a vast stretch of time had vanished between them and they were together again, on the mountainside. Then a shadow touched her eyes, and the moment was gone.

'Jeff got out a bit, then,' Alan said after a short, uneasy silence.

'It was the darts, really,' Marilyn explained. 'After you left the valley, Jeff became quite the local sportsman. As I recall, you were never much for any games, but Jeff was good at them all. He played for the rugby club, and there was cricket in the summer. For a while he was in the basketball team too, when he suddenly started to shoot up. He was tall then, and lean; fit. But then, quite suddenly, he got interested in darts, and after that things changed: he was over the New Inn most nights, and then he joined the darts team, got involved in the valley leagues. He began to put on weight — got a bit stout, as Aunt Matty put it — and as soon as he got home from the factory, he was down the pub and the club, taking anyone on for a game. I asked him once how it was he'd given up the outdoor games for this one — it was the precision, he said. But I think there was more to it than that. It was the challenge, and the excitement of the gambling.'

'How do you mean?'

Marilyn shrugged. 'He wasn't earning much, but there were nights when he'd bet maybe five or six pounds on a game. He always won — well, he lost very rarely, anyway — so it wasn't a problem for him, but I think the *edge* it gave him was the real draw for him. And then, in a little while, other people began to bet on him and it was like — I don't know how I can describe it. A downhill run, faster and faster? The more money people placed on him, the better he seemed to play. It was like a surge of adrenalin, I suppose. He enjoyed the *pressure*, and it improved his darts. It was why Jim hitched on to him. Jim saw it as a rare talent.'

'They were close friends?' Alan asked.

Marilyn hesitated for a few moments before answering. 'I suppose they were, though it was difficult for me to know. Jeff was a very *private* person in many ways, and he became even more private as darts-playing became obsessional with him. In the early days, when he and Jim were playing together in the local team, yes, I suppose they were close friends. Later, I'm not so sure.'

'How do you mean?'

'I'm not sure I can explain it. I've used the word *obsessional*. That was it. Nothing mattered but the darts, to Jeff. The money wasn't so important, not like it always was to Jim. The main thing was to improve his performance in front of the board. And the excitement, the noise, the cheering—he wanted that but not for itself, I believe—he wanted it only for the extra surge it gave his game. You've never seen these occasions?'

Alan shook his head. 'It's a foreign world to me.'

'You ought to go some time. You ought to see Freddy Thomas. In some ways, in the obsessional bit, he's like Jeff. In others, not. Jeff always showed his excitement and his happiness when he was playing well. In the same way, when things were going badly he showed his unhappiness too, like that last time in Swansea. But Freddy's not like that. He never changes. Cold, he is; nothing seems to move him. A machine—committed and . . .' She shuddered slightly. 'Ruthless, I suppose. You get the idea he'd stop at nothing to get what he wanted.'

'And he wanted the same thing as Jeff?'

'I suppose so. To be the best. And Freddy wasn't, of course, not while Jeff was there. Now . . .'

'But I gather your husband and Freddy were in some business organization with Jeff,' Alan said.

She nodded. 'That's right. But it suited all three of

them. Jim wasn't the same standard as they were—but he could handle the business side, appearance money, stakes and so on. It left them free to fight things out at the board. And they pooled winnings, so everyone was happy. As I said, Jeff was never bothered about the money side anyway. Most of what he got I believe he just banked. There was only the car—it was his one extravagance. A yellow Porsche: quite a car.'

She fell silent; perhaps, like Alan, she had a sudden vision of how it must have been that night in the darkness of the mountain road when, headlights blazing, the great yellow sports car would have crashed through the fence above the reservoir.

They sat like that for a little while, staring at the water, concerned with their own private thoughts. Then Marilyn stirred, shivered slightly, and glanced at Alan. 'Anyway, what about you? You've not said much about the way things are with you. I . . . I heard you got married.'

'That's right. Diana Meldon she was, daughter of a Midlands businessman.'

'No children?'

'None.'

'And she's not with you in Bristol?'

Alan looked away, squinting up towards the trees across the stream. The sky was a bright blue, but in the west small white clouds were building up to shadow the morning. 'We're not actually living together at the moment.'

'Oh.' She hesitated. 'I'm not quite sure what that means.'

'Neither am I, exactly.' He managed a wry smile. 'I suppose, if we had discussed it, we'd have called it a trial separation. As it is, since we *didn't* talk about it, there's the possibility it's something more. Called breakdown of marriage.'

'I'm sorry.'

Sorrow. It wasn't something that Alan Fearnley felt. He was still trying to analyse his feelings, but the suspicion was growing inside him that though he could lay claim to sadness at the separation, the greater emotions were concerned with puzzlement.

'It's . . . er . . . none of my business but . . . was there someone else?' Marilyn asked.

'It was something like that,' Alan replied. 'I'm sorry, that sounds vague, but the whole thing is still a bit confusing. I'd looked on the period in Bristol as helpful to sort things out in my mind, and then there was Jeff's death in the paper, and . . . well, I've got a few professional problems as well . . .'

'That's why you were so preoccupied when I joined you.' She considered for a moment. 'With so much to sort out, I imagine you won't be staying around here too long, then.'

Alan stood up, then stretched out a hand to help her to her feet. Her hand was warm in his, and smaller than he had remembered. 'I'm not so sure. I told them at the Bristol office I was taking a week or so off. I'll take the chance to do as Aunt Matty wants, and settle Jeff's affairs, and that'll give me time to sort out the other things in my mind as well. So I shan't be leaving the valley for a little while, at least.'

'I'm glad of that, Alan.' She sounded slightly breathless as she said it, vaguely suprised that the words had come out at all. Alan glanced at her, slightly puzzled, not knowing how to take the comment. It had all been so long ago and now, feeling vulnerable, and with the debris of his last few days with Diana still scattered in his mind, it was no time to ask questions of another woman. He followed Marilyn quietly as she walked ahead of him up the track.

'There's one thing you ought to do,' she was saying, 'and that's not spend too much time with Aunt Matty. If you give her the chance she'll start using you to replace Jeff—and that'll be bad for her when you leave again. Evenings at the house will be pretty gloomy for a while; you know what the neighbours are like: they'll be going in and talking about death with her, and that can be pretty hard to take. They'll be coming in to commiserate, but . . . I think you ought to get out, and see what you've managed to miss up to now.'

'And what might that be?'

'The world that fascinated your brother; the world he ruled in. There's a match in Cardiff tonight. Semi-finals. We're going down—why don't you come?'

'I might very well do that,' Alan said as he walked beside her down the hill.

In the village he called at the local bank and made an appointment to see the manager the following afternoon to discuss his brother's estate, then returned to Aunt Matty's house. She was just about to go out to do some shopping and she asked him what he would like to eat that evening. He was reminded of Marilyn's prediction when he saw the disapproval in her eyes at hearing he would be going out. She demanded to know where he would be, and he hesitated, wanting to refuse to tell her and feeling all the old, insistent domination reaching out to smother him again, as it had all those years ago before he had fled from her and the valley. At last he explained that Jim Carter would be driving down to take Freddy Thomas to the darts semi-finals, and that Alan would be picking up Marilyn to take her down in time for the start. She looked at him for several seconds, but he could not read her expression; then she twisted her mouth and nodded, and walked away down the street to the shop on the corner.

Alan went upstairs to his brother's room.

The furniture there was good and fairly new: some of Jeff's earnings had obviously gone to making his bedroom more comfortable than Alan had remembered. On the chest of drawers in the corner was lined up a group of trophies, presumably from some minor championships which counted for little when compared with the successes denoted in the front room below. The wardrobe had already been cleared of Jeff's clothes by Aunt Matty, but she had placed all Jeff's personal effects in the top drawer of the chest of drawers. They were few enough. His brother, Alan concluded, had not been addicted to material possessions, apart, it seemed, from the yellow Porsche in which he had died. There were a few letters of invitation to various championships over the years, a number of sponsorship requests which suggested that quite a large number of people had wanted to use Jeff's success to promote their business ventures, and there were half a dozen or more presentation boxes of darts, the tools of Jeff Fearnley's trade. Alan wondered which would have been Jeff's favourite set: he would have had one particular set he would always have used. All professionals, in any sport, needed to have tools in which they were confident and a precision sport like darts would require a balance, a familiarity of touch that would make all the difference between success and failure. Alan knew nothing about darts, but he knew the necessity for the pursuit of perfection that Jeff would have felt.

In the second drawer of the chest he found the strongbox. It was made of wood, with an inlay of Indian design, and it was a curious possession to find in Jeff's room. It smelled of spices and it suggested to Alan that maybe his brother had held fanciful dreams unsuspected by Alan or Aunt Matty. Their insubstantiality was, nevertheless, underlined by the existence of no other such object in the room. It might have been a whim of the moment that caused Jeff Fearnley to buy that box—but it did contain the results of his few years at the top of the darts world of the valleys.

There were four insurance policies. They were for two thousand pounds each, with profits, but had not been running very long. The cash valuations in the event of death were nominated. They would bring in something short of ten thousand pounds. Underneath them, Alan found a bank deposit book and a building society deposit book. The local bank was currently holding fifteen thousand pounds and the building society three thousand. Jeff had also filed in the box, with some care, a number of bank statements the last of which showed that he had in his current account some three thousand pounds.

At the bottom of the box, under some letters relating to inland revenue claims and expenses, Alan found Jeff's last will and testament. It was in the necessary legal language and it contained nothing of his brother other than his final intentions, as dictated to the local solicitor. It had been witnessed by two of the neighbours, and it left all his property to Aunt Matty.

Alan sat on the bed, reading the will. It was a strange thing for a young man to do, preparing his will when he was still in his twenties, and then by its terms leaving everything to the elderly aunt who had brought him up. And yet Alan could understand the pressures that would have caused him to do it: making money, and a lot of it; being made to feel his debt to Aunt Matty; being told that if he died she would be left alone and destitute. Some of the pressures would have been subtle, but others would have been direct. Alan sighed: he was already regretting his decision to stay on in the house for a few days — and yet, when he considered the other problems awaiting solution, he knew he was in a dilemma either way.

He made a note of the policy numbers and those of the deposit accounts and then searched through the other drawers. There was nothing more of importance, except for a few share certificates which brought the total up to almost thirty-five thousand pounds. He tied them in a small bundle and then went through the envelopes that were scattered in the top drawer. Most of them contained nothing of importance but in one envelope he found a cheque.

Surprised, he read it carefully. It was in the sum of five thousand pounds, and drawn on an organization called Farrier Enterprises. It had been signed, in a neat, precise hand, by one Charles Edsel, director of Farrier Enterprises. It was dated some five days before Jeff Fearnley had died.

Alan held it in his hand, tapping it against his thumb. He could quite easily have missed the cheque, for it had not been kept in the wooden box with other personal financial effects. He wondered how it was that Jeff had not followed what seemed to be a careful practice of keeping such things together, and he wondered too why it had not been cashed. It was possible that Jeff had forgotten it, but unlikely; it was possible that he had been too busy during the few days before he died to place it to his account. Yet all that would have been required was a letter with the cheque to his bank manager. It was odd, but it made little difference, Alan reasoned. The cheque was still valid: he could take it to the bank tomorrow and have it placed on the deposit account while he checked arrangements to take out probate of the will.

It was, nevertheless, evidence of uncharacteristic behaviour on the part of his dead brother. He knew so little about Jeff, and the kind of man he had become, that the picture he had gained while going through his effects, of a tidy, careful man as far as money and accounts were concerned, was one he had wished to retain—a sharp, clear image of the man he had not seen for fifteen years.

The cheque, unpresented, overlooked, was blurring that image, casting it out of focus in a manner that left Alan vaguely dissatisfied and uneasy.

III

It was an experience quite unlike any other for Alan Fearnley. As soon as he and Marilyn had entered the Black Cat night-club the noise had reached out, washing over them in a great baying sound, crashing and reverberating at its peak but supported by an undertow of constant murmuring. While he waited for Marilyn to emerge from the cloakroom he had been intrigued by the sudden hushed silence before the booming of the microphone; when she joined him he realized, as they walked through the swing doors, that he had to revise his views of the narrowness of the life Jeff had been leading, and of the world of the darts player.

The semi-finals were taking place on the dance floor of the night-club which was packed with small circular tables at which men and women were seated. Some were eating basket meals, others were merely drinking. Mini-skirted waitresses bounced half-bared breasts among the crowded tables, serving drinks, baskets and untouchable sex, but the eyes of the men were fixed on the stage at the far end of the room. Centrally placed on the stage was an advertising board flickering the names of the evening's sponsors and fixed on the structure itself was the focus of attention — the dart board. The stage was lit by a bright pool of light cast from the spotlights high above; at one side stood a small, bespectacled, dinner-jacketed man, hair slicked down, a microphone in his hand. He watched the board with a manic intensity, gesticulating as each dart thudded home. He saw himself as a conductor, an impresario of sound; as Alan and Marilyn stood there the gesticulating arm raised baying approvals from the crowd, and he played them, sharpening the tension, lifting them to a pitch of excited support that would raise the players's games as well as their own enjoyment of the occasion.

Marilyn glanced around the room, checking the tables where the competitors sat. 'There's Jim, with the others. He'll have seats for us.'

She began to thread her way across the crowded room as the little man with the microphone boomed across their heads: '*And now we welcome Big Jimmy from the Outback—will Waltzin' Matilda be the song of the night?*'

He was stepping forward, black-shirted, silver-buttoned, left-handed, a big man with a Zapata moustache and greying dark hair. The Australian was a well-known favourite, for there was a rumbling of approval from contingents to the left, a drumming of feet which fell away only when the first dart flicked into the treble twenty. It was followed by a second precise dart and the Australian shifted slightly on his feet as the microphone boomed: '*There's still room in the bed . . . can he nail a third treble . . . he's* DONE *it . . . one hundred and* EIGHTY! *Can the Midlands Machine follow that?*'

The Midlands Machine waddled forward, shaking his arms like a self-important chicken, loosening the muscular tensions he feared, and Marilyn and Alan approached Jim Carter's table. Carter rose to greet them as the roar about the stage proclaimed that the Midlands Machine was starting his reply in style.

'Alan,' Carter said above the din. 'Glad you could make it. Join us . . . there's a couple of seats here.'

Alan pulled out a chair for Marilyn and sat down himself. Jim Carter ordered some drinks from a blonde, gum-chewing waitress and then concentrated his attention, with others seated at the table, upon the two men on the stage. Big Jimmy and the Midlands Machine—whoever he might be—were throwing their darts with a coldness and possession that seemed to generate enormous excitement in the crowd. Some of it came through to Alan, the mass hysteria of people packed in the room, even though he was but vaguely aware of what was actually happening on the arc-lit stage. But his own growing interest was added to by a realization of the precision involved in the placing of the darts in the board. They flicked through the air, arcing and flashing under the spotlights, their flights gleaming as they thudded into the board, and the microphone boomed out the numbers—one hundred and twenty, one hundred and forty, one hundred and eighty—and Alan knew that the two men on the oche were firing those darts into a tiny space with a mechanical, precise regularity that was almost frightening. Their intensity and commitment was total: and Jeff had been one of these men.

There was a sudden, excited roar and Big Jimmy was turning, raising one hand as he obtained the double eighteen that took him through the first leg of the match. Jim Carter was grinning, looking at Alan and scratching his thick, curly hair. 'Quite a player, Big Jimmy. Came over from Australia last year, and he's coining it now. But Freddy'll be able to take him—either tonight, or in the finals. You've not met Freddy yet, Alan.'

Freddy Thomas was sitting beside Carter, and slightly in front of him, facing the stage. Now he turned his head, looked at Alan and nodded. 'You're Jeff's brother.'

'That's right.'

'Nice to meet you.'

His voice was flat and uninterested, and he turned away again to watch the two men on the stage. Alan could not be certain whether there was deliberate rebuff in the man's behaviour, or whether it was merely a concentration upon the sport that obviously obsessed him as it had Jeff. But as Alan looked at him in semi-profile, noting the lean asceticism of his features, the unfashionably cut, close crop of his hair, the thinness of his mouth and narrowness of his shoulders, he had the feeling that Freddy Thomas was aware of his scrutiny and nervous about it.

'When this match is over there'll be a short interval,' Marilyn was saying in his ear. 'Freddy'll be up then. He's playing Harry Dickson — that's him over there in the white sweater and blue collar — and after that he's got only one more match to get a place in the finals.'

Alan looked at Marilyn. 'Is he likely to make it?'

She smiled. She had good teeth; they flashed whitely at him. 'He's likely to make it.'

And if coolness brought him through, he had enough of that, Alan considered. The players sweated on the stage and the numbers rolled down with an automatic precision; the microphone boomed out its persistent, contrived excitement and the lights and the drink and the drama of the close confrontation at the board brought chanting and shouting and cheering from the packed tables on the floor. But Freddy Thomas sat still, his hands in his lap, glaring as though mesmerized at the pool of light on the stage. It was only when the match was concluded, to a rising crescendo of sound as the Australian finally defeated the Midlands Machine, that he moved, shuddering slightly as though emerging from a cold trance, and turned to sip at the half glass of lager at his elbow. His eyes met Alan's briefly before slipping nervously away: they were cold eyes, thoughtful and controlled, unwilling to be held. The lights were dimming on the stage: the master of ceremonies was declaring the amnesty of a ten-minute break. Men were leaving their tables, walking about, and the excitement was cooling, dying.

'Danny Elias will be here somewhere,' Marilyn said. 'I expect he'll be across at some time — so I should grab the chance to make a bet while you can. Or do accountants know too much about odds ever to bet?'

'I wouldn't say that. But Elias takes bets?'

'That's right. He's got a number of business interests, mainly in the Swansea area, but one of them is a string of betting shops—and he's so hooked on a regular flutter himself that he'll lay you personal odds on anyone you care to name.'

'Except me,' Freddy Thomas said suddenly. 'Not on me, tonight.'

Marilyn smiled thinly. 'You're that confident?'

'There's no one here can take me tonight,' Thomas said. 'Not now.'

His cold eyes flickered quickly and disturbingly towards Alan, as though he was suddenly aware of having said something out of turn. For a moment Alan did not understand, then he realized what had passed through Freddy Thomas's mind: if the Porsche hadn't crashed through that wall, Jeff would be here tonight, disputing Freddy's claim.

Alan sipped the drink brought by the pert-breasted waitress. 'The girls are getting more attention now,' he said, smiling.

'Priorities,' Marilyn agreed, smiling in return. 'When the darts start again, not a man here will even notice the waitresses . . . Did you find Aunt Matty at home when you got back?'

'Ahuh. Then she went shopping.'

'I know. I met her down the street. She . . . she gave me sort of a funny look.'

Alan hesitated. 'I told her I was coming down here with you tonight.' Involuntarily, his glance slipped past her to Jim Carter, engrossed in conversation with a man on the table behind him. 'I don't think she entirely approved.'

'Of going out, or going out with me?'

It was not a question he wanted to answer, and he was even more aware of the presence of her husband, turning back now to their own table. He shrugged. 'I don't know. Anyway, I spent most of the day going through Jeff's things and starting to put matters to rights. Aunt Matty wants me to clear up the estate for her, so I'll check arrangements for probate of Jeff's will.'

'He'll have a fair bit of money to leave,' Jim Carter said, leaning forward across the table, and Freddy Thomas's head turned also, suddenly interested in what was being said. 'Our partnership was pretty good these last three years, and Jeff spent hardly a penny.'

'Mmmm. It looks as though he salted most of it away,' Alan agreed. 'I wondered . . .'

'What about?' Marilyn asked.

'Whether he saw it as a running-away fund.'

There was a short silence as the three people at the table stared at him. He was no longer certain why he had said what he did: it had been half-serious only, and dictated by his own experiences and needs, but he suspected only Marilyn knew that. Carter cleared his throat. 'Running away? From what? He had everything he wanted in the valley.'

'Except freedom,' Marilyn said.

Jim Carter stared at her uncomprehendingly. 'He had all the freedom he wanted. And he was making money. What the hell are you talking about?'

There was an ugly edge in the atmosphere, and Alan suspected that the man and wife were somehow not even talking about Jeff Fearnley, but about themselves. He picked up his drink. 'It was a stupid remark. The fact is, *I* found living in the valley a stifling experience, and I had to get out. I suppose I just wondered whether Jeff had ever felt the same way—and when I saw the manner in which he'd been saving his money . . .'

'No.' Jim Carter shook his head. 'He had no intention of leaving. He was comfortable at home; our partnership was heading for big things; it was the lifestyle he wanted.' He paused, looked around him. '*This* was what he wanted. You should have seen him in these kinds of surroundings, Alan. He was *magic*.'

Freddy Thomas's eyes were fixed on Jim Carter. Something moved in those eyes, deep and angry, as though Thomas felt he would never remove the ghost of the better darts player from his mind. He stood up abruptly, and said in a harsh tone, 'We'd better get organized.'

'Right.' Jim Carter grinned at Alan. 'Takes a few minutes to set things up, see. We'll need to get over nearer the stage, and we'll need a table for the beer. Freddy likes to have a few halves lined up—keeps him cool, a few glasses of Carlsberg, and keeps the tension drowned. Jeff was the same.'

'But with him it was Newcastle Brown. Four to set himself up, and three to replace the sweat he lost during the tournament—that right, Jim?' It was Danny Elias, flashing his professional smile, oozing bonhomie and ready to slip into Jim Carter's chair as he rose. He was dressed in grey slacks, open-necked blue shirt and blue jacket, and he was at ease, at home in these surroundings. 'Good night so far,' he announced. 'Had fifty on Big Jimmy and three fools to take the odds. But there's no way I'll take anyone on with *this* match. That right, Freddy?'

Thomas glanced back at Elias, as he walked away. 'One horse race,' he said laconically.

Danny Elias shook his head. 'I reckon he's right, too. The kind of form he's in at the moment, no one'll touch him. Jeff, now . . .' He hesitated, flicking a sidelong glance at Alan. 'Jeff would've still been able to take him, I reckon. He had a kind of hoodoo on Freddy, you know that? Even when Freddy was on song, and Jeff's form indifferent, *somehow* Jeff always came through when it mattered. Freddy would be finding the wire at important times, losing scores. It was odd. No, it was always Jeff . . . except for the once. Anyway,' he said, turning to Marilyn, 'how's things with you, chick? Jim keeping you happy?'

She smiled mechanically; the question was a rhetorical one but Alan noted the way in which Elias's glance slipped over Marilyn's shoulders and breasts. Though he had no rights in the matter, Alan felt vaguely annoyed. He looked away, towards the stage where Carter was arranging some bottles on the table at the side of the apron. Freddy Thomas was walking up on to the stage, the man earlier identified as Harry Dickson just behind him. Dickson was immaculately turned out in a white sweater with blue collar, and red armbands gleamed above powerful biceps. The overall effect was somewhat spoiled by the beer paunch that jutted massively under the white sweater, but standing beside Freddy Thomas, small, lean, soberly dressed, he looked solidly confident.

The man with the microphone was introducing the two men to the audience and there was a deafening reception for each, cheering mingling with catcalls. Alan turned to speak to Marilyn but she gestured — they were about to start the game. The man with the microphone boomed out: *'And here we have the wee Welshman against Goliath Harry Dickson. A match to remember, and it's Harry to go first!'*

Elias leaned across, grinning. 'Big advantage, throwing first. Means Freddy'll be chasing his tail all the while. But just watch Freddy go.'

The first darts thudded into the board, the crowd howled ecstatically at the microphone's excited top score, and within minutes Alan found himself caught up in the fervour and tension of the hall. For the first time he began to appreciate the extent of the skills being demonstrated on the stage. It was not merely the precision with which they flicked the darts into the board; there was also the speed of calculation, as the blend of figures and numbers changed. He knew it would be the result of long years of practice, so that the combinations would occur automatically as the numbers rose, but even so, as the players went for configurations of trebles and doubles he admired their speed of reaction. There was no pause for thought: the microphone boomed, the spotlight harshened the shadows, and behind them the baying, roaring crowd was ignored, as each man took his turn, and displayed his own peculiar characteristics and skills.

Dickson was at the oche, a quick twirl of the first dart before throwing. *'And it's fifty-six Harry needs,'* clamoured the man with the microphone. *'Just a sixteen and double top.'* The dart flashed. *'He's hit the wire,'* crooned the microphone. *'Is his concentration gone?'* The second dart thudded into the board. *'There's the sixteen . . . and* THERE'S THE DOUBLE TOP, FOLKS!'

Harry Dickson was slapping one elbow in triumph and turning, grinning, as the fishbowl of half-drunken enthusiasts raised their glasses and howled exultantly. Freddy Thomas was already at the oche, squinting at the board, and then, as the yelling died, he began the next game, his earnestness bringing out beads of sweat on his forehead, using the peculiar crab-like shuffle Alan had noted earlier, as he sought new flight paths for his dragon-flighted darts.

'Not a good start,' Elias conceded, 'but the boy will make it . . . and it gives the crowd a thrill.'

'Are they always like this?' Alan asked, smiling around at the excited crowd.

'Didn't use to be, but of recent years, as the TV crews have moved in and the money's got big, it's sort of become a kind of Roman circus. And believe me—those boys up on the stage, they bleed as much as the old gladiators did. All right, it's *inside*, but don't think of what they're doing as just a sport. They're sweating blood and guts, I tell you. And not just one night. When they're on the circuit, like Freddy, it can be three, four nights a week. And that's apart from locals, and exhibitions, and practices.'

'A programme like that would mean a considerable

amount of travelling,' Alan remarked, raising his voice to cope with the howling that greeted another series from Freddy Thomas.

'You can say that again.'

'Jeff was on the circuit, I suppose.'

The look that Elias gave him had an almost derisive quality. 'On it? He almost *was* the bloody circuit! Jeff was the man to beat. Over the last two years you couldn't get near prize money unless you either beat Jeff or missed meeting him until the finals. The wonder was, Freddy never seemed to face him until the later stages — or Jeff would have sunk him earlier on. My guess is, Jim Carter persuaded most managements to use a seeding system, and *arrange* a draw that didn't put those two into contention until late on. Put his back into things, Jim did.' He paused, glanced towards Marilyn. 'Hey, that reminds me. I knew there was something odd. That suit Jim's wearing —'

'Superstition,' Marilyn said shortly, almost warningly. Alan glanced towards Jim Carter where he stood near to stage: he was wearing a powder blue suit, dark blue tie and white shirt. He turned back to Marilyn enquiringly.

She raised a shoulder, shrugging. 'Jim's had a thing these last few years, while Jeff was at the top.'

'Always wore the same suit — a check thing —'

'It was garish.'

'But it seemed to do the trick,' Elias remonstrated, grinning. 'His luck suit, he said, always wore it on nights when Jeff and Freddy were throwing. Brought luck to the partnership, he reckoned. But now —'

'He got rid of it,' Marilyn said shortly.

Elias frowned. 'What do you mean?'

Her eyes slipped towards Alan. She hesitated. 'When Jeff died in that crash, Jim felt it wasn't . . . appropriate to wear it any more. So he destroyed it. The lucky charm was gone. The last time he wore it was at the Swansea match.' She nodded towards her husband near the stage. 'He's hoping *that* suit will prove lucky now.'

It seemed odd that a man like Jim Carter should prove to be superstitious in that way, but Alan reflected that the unreal world of darts might encourage that sort of calling to the gods. A tiny piece of luck could make all the difference — and luck had certainly played its part in the match at Swansea.

'Was Jeff playing the circuit during the week before he died?' Alan asked suddenly.

Elias grimaced. 'He was. Night he died, it was a big night and he'd been working up to it all week, with exhibitions up in the Midlands and North Wales. He wanted that title . . . but why do you ask?'

'I just got the impression he didn't have much time on his hands that week.'

'Time for what?'

Alan shrugged. 'To visit the bank. But it's of no importance.'

The crowd was baying. Thomas had taken the second game and Harry Dickson was pushing forward, a belligerent scowl on his face. Beside him, impassive, Freddy Thomas waited his turn.

During the next half-hour Alan lost himself in the tension of the match. Despite Elias's predictions and Thomas's own confident air, Dickson was proving to be a better fighter than they had given him credit for. The match was finely balanced: the games clicked away and after the completion of two legs the players were level. And Dickson took the first game in the final, deciding leg.

Freddy Thomas's lean, ascetic features seemed unmoved. His cold eyes were glistening with concentration and commitment; he had eliminated all unnecessary movement, the darts flying with the merest blurred flick of his wrist, the dragon-flights whirring from the swift movement of his hand, and as the tension rose and perspiration gleamed on the faces of the two players at the oche there was a change in the atmosphere about them, beyond the stage. For suddenly the noise had dropped, the solid *plunk* of the darts being the only sound in the hall until the throaty roar that greeted each announcement of the score. Freddy Thomas took the second game and the third; a sneer of arrogance touched his mouth as he made way for Dickson in the fourth game, but the big man wasn't finished: he began well, stringing together a series of scores, none of which fell below one hundred, and Freddy was trailing after a poor second attempt. When Dickson, sweating profusely, finished with a flourish to get sixty-seven, with a seventeen, twenty and double fifteen, chairs were overturned and beer glasses crashed as the room rose to him. He had levelled the scores, and there was pandemonium in the hall. Elias turned an excited, grinning face towards Marilyn.

'Maybe I should have put some money on this one after all! Dickson's playing above himself tonight.'

But Alan was watching Freddy Thomas. The slight figure was slightly hunched, head lowered, staring at his feet as though searching there for inspiration. But when he raised his head and glanced sideways at the cheering crowd Alan saw the cold concentration in the man's eyes. This wasn't a game for Thomas: it might be fame or recognition he was after, or maybe it was the prospect of money to be won, but Alan doubted that. There was something else. Freddy Thomas *cared* too much. There was an iron burning in his soul, and for a moment the hairs on the back of Alan's neck prickled as he thought suddenly of Jeff. His brother had played this man night after night, and had held the edge on him, beating him regularly. But as Alan saw the commitment in the man's eyes now, with the match with Dickson all square, he wondered how Jeff and Thomas could ever have remained friends. Freddy Thomas could never have ac-

cepted Jeff's superiority—and yet he must have held that
iron in check. As Thomas threw the first dart, Alan
glanced quickly at Marilyn. Her eyes met his, and he felt
she recognized the puzzle in his mind. But he doubted
whether she would have the answer.

Perhaps even Freddy Thomas had no answer.

The room was now completely silent, the way it had
used to be, apparently, when Jeff was throwing, but it was
an aching silence, spring-loaded with tension. Thomas
was shifting his stance, leaning forward on balanced hips,
calculating distance and angle, and then the dragon-
flighted darts, his sole concession to flamboyance, were
flashing to the board, thudding satisfyingly, presaging
the crescendo of sound from the audience.

*'That's what they call pressure darts, folks—from
mind, to hand, to board! And it's Goliath Harry Dickson
to play again and it's still anybody's match!'*

But it wasn't. Alan's glance slipped around the room at
the sweating, excited, grinning faces—a predominantly
male, hard-drinking audience, a scattering of somewhat
tousled women with apparently standard gin-and-tonics,
and though they seemed to regard the issue as still in
doubt, Alan thought otherwise. Tyro he might be,
unknowledgeable about the sport, he yet was convinced
that Harry Dickson would find it impossible to beat
Freddy Thomas tonight. And as the next few minutes
slipped past it became obvious. The big man was playing
well, but the deadly accuracy of Freddy Thomas's play
was destructive of Dickson's confidence and control. The
top scores rolled away under Thomas's arm and even
though he faltered briefly, just once, when his second
dart hit the wire and bounced out, the mechanical precision returned with just one hundred and forty-three to
play for. The silence was a solid, heavy, controlled excitement as Thomas leaned forward, hand poised, eyes glittering. The dart arced through the space and *plunked* in

the board. '*Treble twenty*!' A ripple of subdued noise ran through the room. The second dart flew and Harry Dickson moved uneasily, peering at the board. '*Treble fifteen*!' There was a brief drumming of feet, hastily overcome. Thomas did his crab shuffle, measuring distance and height, moving up on the board. There was not a whisper in the room, and even Alan held his breath. The barely perceptible flick of the wrist and the dragon-flighted dart flashed in the air: there was a pause, a rumble in the microphone throat and then a gasp. '*And he's done it*—DOUBLE NINETEEN! *Going out in style . . .*' The rest of the professional comment was lost in the wave of cheering that burst over the room as men rose, punching fists in the air and yelling Freddy Thomas's name.

Alan looked at Marilyn. Her face was flushed, her eyes warm and excited, and she laughed in his direction, caught up in the infection that had spread throughout the room. Freddy Thomas, in spite of his personal coldness, was at this moment a folk hero, a man to admire for his professional skills, talents that could generate passion in everyone present and make him seem, for a little while, a demi-god in this darkened, smoke-wreathed room.

Thomas was standing on the stage, arms raised, a half-smile on his face, but the glitter in his eyes seemed to Alan to be the only real thing about the man at this moment. It was more than triumph; it was knowledge, too. And he wondered how Jeff had used to react, to success, and adulation, and the pulsing excitement of a roaring crowd.

Danny Elias turned, his face flushed. 'Well, that's good enough to see Freddy through to the finals next week. There'll be more than a few bob riding on him then, but the odds won't be good. Can't see anyone getting near him, but for the Australian.'

'It was a fairly close run thing tonight,' Marilyn demurred.

Elias shook his head. 'I don't reckon. You notice how

Freddy sharpened his game in that last leg? He's bloody cold enough to deliberately let Harry Dickson into the game, just to hype himself up into a match, know what I mean? Freddy's never been a percentage player—and he enjoys the *needle*. I think he'll have dangled a carrot in front of Harry tonight—just to have the pleasure of snatching it away in the last game.'

'He's that confident?' Alan asked.

Danny Elias stared at him for a few moments, then nodded. 'The only time I've ever seen Freddy play percentage darts was against Jeff—and even then, it did him no good. In fact, I used to think it was Jeff who allowed Freddy in, from time to time, the way Freddy did Harry Dickson tonight. Just to squash him when the time came.' He nodded again. 'Aye, Freddy'll have learned that little play from your brother.'

Alan looked across to the stage where Freddy was stepping down to Jim Carter's congratulations. Behind him stood Harry Dickson, unable to hide the scowl of disappointment caused by his defeat. But as Alan watched, Thomas turned back and said something to Dickson, and the big man's features darkened, a flush of anger scarring his face, twisting his mouth. Freddy Thomas had demonstrated his ascendancy over the big man; now, it seemed, he had rubbed salt in the wound with some well-chosen gibe. At that moment, Harry Dickson hated Freddy Thomas.

Yet Freddy and Jeff Fearnley had been friends.

Alan turned back to Elias. 'You tended to support Jeff at these matches?' he asked.

'With hard cash, boy, hard cash. The odds were never very good of recent months,' Elias said, 'but what's the point in backing a loser?'

Freddy Thomas had been a loser, but not now.

Elias was rising. He put a familiar hand on Marilyn's shoulder and squeezed; she responded with a faint smile and Elias grinned at Alan, leaving the table to make way for Jim Carter and the returning hero, as the next pair of players climbed on stage. Elias waved to Thomas, then punched Alan playfully on the shoulder before walking back to his own table. Forced to stand to let him pass, Alan then stepped back to allow a perspiring waitress to squeeze in front of him with drinks for a nearby table. As he did so he rocked the table behind him and turned to apologize. He looked up, to the back of the room, and there was a man standing against the wall, beer glass in his hand, staring in Alan's direction.

He seemed to be alone, standing apart from the throng of tables, and for one long moment in time his eyes held Alan's, almost questioningly. Then his glance slipped away and he turned, walking towards the bar as Alan sat down. Marilyn was pushing her chair closer to Alan's as Freddy Thomas and Jim Carter returned in triumph, amid much back-slapping. Men crowded around the table, shouting approval of the last match and Thomas's pale features were animated for the first time, as he glowed in the congratulations showered on him. But Alan was frowning: images moved in his head, far removed from this room. The man against the wall, who had been staring at him: he had seen him somewhere before. Briefly he caught the image, but then it danced away again even as he grasped for it.

It was only much later, when he was lying, sleepless, in the narrow room in Aunt Matty's house he had known ever since he was a boy, that he remembered where he had seen the man before. The darkness about him was warm and heavy; its airlessness brought the sweat out on his body, making him think of the close confines of the grave.

And he remembered that he had seen the man just a few days previously, at the cemetery, on the day that Jeff was buried.

IV

Alan spent the following morning making several phone calls to business and professional contacts in the company and accountancy worlds: fortunately, one of the extravagances which Jeff had indulged in was three telephones in Aunt Matty's house, so he was able to place his calls undisturbed. The results of his calls left him uneasy in mind, however, for they amounted to confirmations of some of his suspicions regarding the role played by Emburey Associates in the dealings of Sunski and Fernline International. At midday Aunt Matty called him to lunch, and he found himself faced by a cooked meal of the kind she had always provided for Jeff. 'He was a big eater,' she explained, 'and you look as if you ought to follow in his footsteps.'

Her attitude towards Alan had changed subtly in the short time he had been at the house. The resentment was still there, and the disapproval, but it was now layered under a softer, more insidious inquisitiveness that presaged, he suspected, an acceptance of Alan Fearnley back into the fold. The fact he had no desire to return to that fold, with all its suffocating possessiveness, was not something he could explain to Aunt Matty; she, for all her perceptiveness, seemed not to understand this, or even recognize it. Perhaps she didn't want to see it. She merely wanted Jeff back; and Alan, in spite of his earlier defection, would have to do as a replacement. So, now, she wanted to know what he was doing, where he was going, what lay in the future, in Bristol, in the Midlands, and in his marriage.

About the last, to her barely concealed resentment, he was not prepared to speak. He told her about Diana, for the two women had never met, but he went very little beyond the physical description of a medium height, fair-haired woman with blue eyes and smooth manners, private school educated, and socially acceptable in the upper echelons of business-backed family life in the Midlands. Aunt Matty sniffed. 'What did you want to go and marry an *English* girl for, then? What's wrong with your own kind? And where is she now, then? Why isn't she looking after you in Bristol?'

These were questions he was not prepared to answer. They were too personal, too close, and too confused in his own mind to allow discussion with the aunt from whose domination he had fled fifteen years previously. His relationships with the women in his life, he considered gloomily, had been far from smooth.

In the afternoon he went to see the bank manager in the village.

Short, rotund, barrel-chested and balding, he could have passed for the typical miner he would have been, perhaps, a generation earlier, if his father had not opened a small shop in the village and ensured that his son did not go down the pit. Now, in his fifties, Mr Lloyd was regarded as a pillar of the local community: still a chapel-goer at a time when chapel support was dwindling in the valley, with one son a doctor and the other a lawyer, he was regarded with respect and pride by the members of the community and not least by himself. Self-made, in his eyes, and a maker of doctors and lawyers in addition, he could feel a warmth based on equality towards Alan Fearnley, even if, at the same time, it was tinged with echoes of resentment that Alan had sought his fortune away from the valley.

'I always feel,' he said as he leaned back in his chair and folded his hands over his comfortable paunch, 'that boys owe a certain . . . *duty*, if you like, to the community they are brought up in — or at least, to the land that nurtured them. My son Owen, now, he's a doctor over at Merthyr, and Glyn — that's my other boy — he's practising in Cardiff. Neither far from his roots, you see, and paying back, in a sense, some of the nourishment they obtained from their growing to manhood in the valley here. Of course, you, well, you had to take your chances outside, didn't you? I understand that. But now you're back — '

'I'm not coming back to work,' Alan interrupted. 'Just to settle my brother's estate, really.'

'Ah, I see. Well, pity it is, because I always like to see local boys come back, make their mark like my boys are doing. But it's all about opportunities, really, isn't it? And your brother, now . . .' Mr Lloyd paused, contemplated his fingers for a moment, searching for the right words. 'He . . . ah . . . he carved out his own opportunities, didn't he? Tragic that he should have died so young, because he showed a certain *acumen* in building up his assets against the day when his . . . ah . . . skill might desert him, you know?'

It was obvious that Mr Lloyd held his greatest admiration for the professional classes, but was not above a grudging respect for entrepreneurs with lesser talents — provided they left their money in his bank. 'You've got an up-to-date statement now of Jeff's holdings?' Alan asked.

One pudgy hand reached forward and tapped the folder on the desk in front of Mr Lloyd. 'It's all in here. He kept a deposit account, and took our advice on share-holdings . . . but it's all in here. He was a cautious man with his money, Jeff Fearnley, and now it's not he who will enjoy the fruits of his labours.' His little eyes regarded Alan curiously. 'I am one of the executors of his will, of course, and matters of probate can really be left to me.'

'I know that, Mr Lloyd. It's merely that Aunt Matty wants me to speed things along a little — and wants me to help in the settlement of the estate.'

Somewhat stiffly, Mr Lloyd said, 'I understand that,

but these things cannot be hurried, as you will know. And all the appropriate steps were taken. The house does not fall into the estate, of course: it is in your aunt's name, even though your brother it was who bought up the freehold for her three years ago. He . . . he looked after her very well, you know.'

What Mr Lloyd really meant was that he knew she had dominated Jeff the way she would have dominated Alan, had he stayed. Alan nodded. 'And the rest—'

'The rest of his possessions was the subject of an inventory,' Mr Lloyd interrupted, 'which you'll find in the folder. Strictly speaking, of course, I'm under no obligation to . . .'

He let the words die away, meaningfully. Alan reached into the inside pocket of his jacket and brought out his wallet. 'I've no doubt you went through the personal effects after the death?'

'Well, no,' Mr Lloyd said. 'His assets at the bank and elsewhere, of course, but it wasn't seemly to intrude on your aunt, and as for his personal effects, well, there wouldn't be much that . . .' He began to turn slightly pink under Alan's steady gaze. 'I mean, it would be going to your aunt anyway, under the will, so I didn't think it necessary . . .'

'*I* went through his personal effects,' Alan said. 'It's just as well, really. I found this.' Carefully, he laid the uncashed cheque in front of Mr Lloyd. The pinkness in the bank manager's cheeks deepened as he read the amount stated on the cheque, and noted its date. He looked up as Alan went on, 'I think, as executor, you ought to arrange for encashment of this cheque immediately: it's a significant amount of money to fall into the estate—which otherwise might have been lost.'

'I don't know how this could have been overlooked by my clerks,' Mr Lloyd began to bluster.

'I do,' Alan said. 'You just didn't ask them to go

through Jeff's personal effects. But no matter. Will you now present the cheque, please, and then I'll call again for an account before probate. Even though—' he smiled disarmingly—'you're under no obligation to me, since I'm not a beneficiary. But I *am* acting for Aunt Matty, so . . .'

'I'll ring you,' Mr Lloyd said coolly, 'once the matter is settled. Good day, Mr Fearnley.'

After all, Alan Fearnley had no account in *his* bank, so why should *he* be polite to a man who not only called his competence into question but also showed no desire to live and work in the valley that had nurtured him?

At eight o'clock that evening Alan had parked his car and was waiting for Marilyn in the bar she had suggested in Cardiff. He was slightly uneasy, for he was not certain what he was doing here. The conversation when they were leaving the night-club the previous night had been short, but somehow pointed, and deliberate. Jim Carter had gone to get his coat and Marilyn was waiting to be driven home: as Alan had taken his leave of her, she had put one hand on his arm.

'Will you be busy tomorrow?'

'Just seeing the bank manager in the afternoon.'

'I wonder whether we could meet in the evening?'

His hesitation had been brief. 'I suppose so.'

'I'm taking the car to Cardiff to do some shopping, and see some friends. Jim is going with Freddy Thomas to Pontardawe. We could have dinner maybe.'

'In Cardiff?'

'About eight.'

She had just had time to nominate the bar before Jim returned and they said goodnight. Since then, Alan had had time to think about the meeting and he was not sure it was wise: there was a furtiveness about it which raised questions in his mind, and in a way reopened old issues that had long since faded. On the other hand, maybe he was over-reacting. With her husband away, maybe Marilyn simply didn't want the prospect of a lonely evening—and what more natural than that she would want the company of an old friend she hadn't seen for fifteen years?

But when he saw her enter the bar and walk towards his table some of the unspoken anxieties touched Alan again, for she had obviously taken some care with her appearance. The dress was new, and emphasized her figure; her eyes were sparkling as though with anticipation and subdued excitement, the kind of excitement that fed off a clandestine appointment; and when she kissed him in welcome there was a pressure of her fingers on his arm that carried meaning. The light touch of her perfume lingered with him as he went up to the bar and bought her a gin and tonic.

Nevertheless, any trepidation or anxiety he felt was soon dispelled. When they left the bar, and went to the restaurant she suggested, the drinks had relaxed him; a good bottle of wine completed the effect and her obvious pleasure at being with him was flattering enough to allow him to enjoy the occasion thoroughly. They talked of inconsequentialities: of old days when they had both been young, of the mountains, of golden Saturday evenings as the sun went down, and for a little while they were both young again.

'But then, you're at least five years younger than I am anyway,' he said, laughing.

'At least,' she agreed, and grinned back with a hint of wickedness. 'Which means you took advantage of me when I was only just at the age of consent.'

'As far as I remember, you were more than merely consenting.'

'That,' she said in mock primness, 'is something you should not remind a lady about.'

Brandies with their coffee made them agree, additionally, that it would be unwise to return to their cars immediately, so since it was a warm, luminous night, they decided to take a short stroll towards the Sophia Gardens, beyond the castle. The trees were massive and black against the sky and the castle loomed behind them; the level green of the sward gleamed in the moonlight, and Marilyn held his arm closely against her breast as they strolled along the pathway.

'You've said nothing at all about your wife,' she murmured after a short silence.

'She's not been on my mind.'

'I'm not sure what that means.'

'Neither am I.' He hesitated, but the alcohol in his veins had made its contribution towards recklessness, and besides, in the warm darkness it seemed right to confide in the woman walking beside him. 'I suppose it means, or *could* mean, that she no longer looms large in my life or my conscious thoughts. But I suppose that's not really true—certainly she was very much on my mind when I left Bristol to come to Jeff's funeral.'

'So what else could it mean?'

'Possibly that in your company she is . . . driven away.'

Marilyn was silent for a while, but the pressure on his arm grew tighter. At last she sighed. 'It's odd, isn't it, how people can grow apart. Is that what's happened with you?'

'I'm not sure. Something like that . . . or something more fundamental, I suspect. It's not so much a question of growing apart as of finding that the person you're married to has always held values different from your own. There's nothing wrong in the fact of it; it's the knowledge that comes after assuming other views . . . your own views . . . were held that amounts to the shock.'

'Views?'

'About personal relationships,' he said flatly.

'Mmmm. *I* think . . . I think you've been hurt, Alan Fearnley.'

'I don't know that I really want—'

'*Was* it another man?'

The question was too direct and too brutal when the wound was still open, ready to bleed again. He was not yet certain whether the bleeding was a washing away of the pain or a dangerous ebbing away of his confidence and control; he was not yet certain whether he wanted truly to face up to the facts that Diana's conduct underlined. She had said she had done it to support him, help him in his career, and such a reason for infidelity was so numbing to him that he had been unable to argue with her. Only later, when anger had broken through, after they had quarrelled violently and he had used the words that had caused her to walk out on him, only then had he tried to bring rationality into the situation, and weigh up what his marriage had been, and what it and his business career meant to him. And he had failed even in that attempt: it had led to his grateful acceptance of the audit in Bristol, and now when problems had loomed there, to his flight to the valley.

For he saw that for what it was now: a flight from realities he was unable to face in Bristol. Yet the paradox was that he was burying himself, briefly, in a world he had already deserted. Perhaps it was an attempt to find a peace that he had always felt *should* have been there, in the valley—even though he had never found it as a young man.

'I can understand,' Marilyn said quietly, 'if you don't want to talk about it. But there's danger too, in keeping things bottled up inside for too long. Maybe, if I had said more at the beginning, things would have been easier now.' She laughed shortly. 'You're not the only one with troubles, you see.'

'Your husband?'

She glanced about her at the moonlit lawns and the dark mass of the trees. She shook her head, almost in regret. 'Ridiculous, isn't it? Walking here in the darkness like a couple of kids, trying to recapture something that disappeared a long time ago. Both went our own ways, we did; you left the valley, and I got married to Jim Carter. Funny; I can't really remember what it was like then—though I was still thinking of you, off and on. But Jim was . . . attentive, I suppose the word was, and I thought I could do worse. And it was all right at first.' She shivered slightly, and drew closer to him, tightening her grip on his arm. 'But then things changed. Or maybe I did. He spent more and more time at the clubs, and when he got involved with Freddy Thomas and Jeff, well, it all became an obsession with him. It meant we never saw each other in the evenings unless I came to the matches, and then, when they started travelling, well, we couldn't afford for me to go as well. Until, finally, he started staying away at night . . . when he didn't need to.'

They had reached a pathway that skirted the lawns and headed out towards Llandaff. Alan stopped. 'We'd better turn back.'

She was standing facing him. She nodded, but made no attempt to move. The silence grew about them, disturbed only by a soft whispering breeze that ruffled the long grass under the trees. Quietly Alan said, 'I think this is a mistake, Marilyn.'

'Maybe. Or maybe we made the mistake years ago, is that it?'

She kissed him. It spun him back through the years and it was as though he could smell the crushed fern again and her skin was as soft and smooth as it had been in the sunlight on the hillside. They stood close after a little while, not speaking, but each of them aware of the trembling that had touched her, and then Alan put his arm around her waist, gently but firmly moving her away, back across the lawns.

'It's time we went back.'

'He's got another woman, Alan. There's no need to feel that it would be a betrayal. He visits her when he's anywhere within striking distance of Neath, and—'

'It's not that,' Alan interrupted. He took a deep breath. 'I'm confused. I've got things to straighten out in my mind, and I don't want—'

'Don't see me as a problem,' she said a trifle coolly. 'I never was the clinging type. There was something good between us years ago, and you broke it up when you left the valley, but I'm not fool enough to think *that* old flame can be rekindled. We're older, and can surely use the maturity we've gained to . . . enjoy our lives, without looking over shoulders for problems.'

'It's not as simple as that, Marilyn.' But he could not explain it to her, because he was unable, yet, to explain it to himself. He felt he had come to a watershed in his life: decisions he took during the next few days could irrevocably change his future. The confusions that underlay his indecisiveness were a mixture of professional and personal problems that had been unalleviated by his return to the valley. He had not *expected* that this return would have cleared his mind, but he had hoped that it would provide breathing space, thinking space. Instead of which the first dullness that had affected his nerveends at the thought of Jeff's death was now wearing off; old, half-buried guilts were re-emerging—towards Aunt Matty, and the brother he had left behind. And Marilyn too: it was another guilt he did not want to sharpen.

They were silent as they walked back to the cars.

'Will I see you soon?' she asked as he opened her car door for her. 'Jim'll be away for a couple of days this week—and the nights get lonely.'

The last words had been said flippantly, with a smile, but they hovered too close to the precipice of truth to be taken too lightly. 'I'll be around, Marilyn, but—'

'Don't say it. Rejection is easier to take when it's not put into words.'

'It's not about rejection,' he said.

She stared at him for a little while, then smiled slightly, nodded. 'No, perhaps you're right. And it's better to move slowly—let both of us get our bearings a bit. See you soon, love.'

She kissed him lightly on the mouth, got in her car and drove away.

Alan returned to his own car, parked in the sidestreet, and took the road for the valley. As he drove away, headlights flickered up behind him, then dimmed. They stayed some sixty yards behind him as he drove out of the city.

Alan could not be certain at what point of time he began to get edgy about the car behind him. He was not bothered by the dimmed headlights—in the city streets he hardly noticed them, and on the valley road they fell back as other, faster cars occasionally moved in between them. But the stationing of the car behind bothered him: it seemed to keep a regulation distance between them, slowing when he slowed, picking up speed when he drove faster. At Pontypridd he thought the car had turned off, but within half a mile it had reappeared again—not that he could be *certain*, for all he could make out was the headlights, but the distance, and the regularity, remained the same.

When he came over the top of the hill it began to rain and the lights of the valley below glittered and danced, refracted on his windscreen. He glanced in his mirror: the headlights kept their station in the darkness along the deserted road. Suddenly, impatiently, Alan braked, pulled in at the side, where the hill sloped up to his left, clumped with sparsely-foliaged trees, bent like old men under the prevailing wind of the bare slopes, and he glared again in his rear mirror. The car behind him began to loom closer, then it too stopped. Seconds ticked away but the car behind came no closer; like Alan's, it was now parked, pulled in under the hillside.

Alan waited, but the occupant of the car behind made no move. Anger touched Alan Fearnley and he opened the car door; as he did so the headlights of the vehicle behind died. Alan left his own car door open and walked back towards the vehicle that had followed him from Cardiff. His step was measured and controlled, but the anger that moved him was also tinged with something else, a touch of fear that sharpened his senses, made his nerve-ends tingle with anticipation. He paused at the car bonnet; he could only vaguely make out the form of the man behind the driving wheel. He was alone.

Alan moved to stand beside the driver's door. He reached down and grasped the door handle: the door was unlocked. The rain in the air was now more than a mere drizzle and he felt its wet fingers in his hair. He pulled the door open and as he did so the courtesy light clicked on, so he could see the features of the man behind the wheel.

He stared at him for several seconds, uncomprehendingly. He was not a complete stranger, for Alan had seen him twice before—at the Black Cat night-club, and at Jeff's funeral. Each time their eyes had met, and each time Alan had wondered about this man. Now the man's narrow features were averted, his eyes staring blankly at the dark road ahead and the tail-lights of Alan's car.

'You've been following me,' Alan said harshly, his voice rasping in the silence.

The narrow head turned, and the man looked at Alan. He could read nothing in the glance, and the stranger, gripping the car wheel tightly, made no reply.

'*Who are you?*' Alan demanded.

For a moment the man seemed to hesitate, as though reluctant, scared to speak. Then he bobbed his head nervously. 'My . . . my name is Nick Edwards.'

It was a light voice, high-pitched with nervousness, and it gave Alan strength, increased his anger in an inexplicable way. He reached out, tugged at the man's shoulder, pulled at his jacket. 'What do you want with me?'

The man struggled ineffectually against Alan's grip, twisting his head away. 'I only . . . I only wanted to know why you'd come back to the valley.'

'What is it to you, for God's sake?' Alan said fiercely. 'I don't know you!'

The eyes suddenly flickered at him, obsessive anger and hate bringing them to life in the darkness. Alan released his grip and Nick Edwards leaned sideways, thrusting his narrow face towards Alan. 'No, you don't know me — but I wanted to know you. And I wanted to know if you'd come back to find out who murdered your brother Jeff!'

CHAPTER 3

I

As they had driven through the valley and up along the winding road of the Bwlch-y-Clawdd the rain had increased in intensity, the wind driving slanting sheets of water across the road in a roaring darkness. Inside the car, Alan Fearnley was aware of the rhythmic beat of the windscreen-wipers and the winking red gleam of Nick Edwards's tail-lights ahead of him, but his mind was numb with shock and his hands gripped the driving wheel tightly, knuckles gleaming white in the faint glow inside the car. Behind him was the steep, falling darkness of the mountain, the lights of the valley floor blotted out by the rain, and in their long climb up the mountain only two cars passed them, white bow-waves of water surging under the headlights as they negotiated the twisting bends of the roadway. Otherwise, it was as though they were in a high, black world where only the teeming rain and the gleam of the catseyes in the road reminded them of reality: a lost, ghostly time, suspended above the world in a blackness that heightened the fantasies now chasing through Alan's mind.

The pace of the car quickened; they were coming out of the bend above the reservoir where he had stopped, before Jeff's funeral, and Edwards, ahead of him, was driving up towards the long, gentler run to the top of the mountain, and the branch forks towards Swansea and Llantrisant. But Edwards would not go beyond the forks — Alan was sure of that. He had suggested they talked where Jeff had died, and Jeff had died on the slope above the reservoir.

To his right Alan was now aware of the beetling rock at the top of the gradient: fifty yards ahead would be the fork to Swansea and even as he realized it he saw the brake lights of Edwards's car glow redly. The car ahead slowed, then turned in a wide U-turn; as Alan drew level he caught sight of Edwards's pale face glaring at him through the side window. Then he himself was turning, to follow Edwards back down the mountain road.

He had expected the man would carry on right down to the sharp bend above the reservoir, but the brake lights glowed again near the lay-by carved under the overhanging rock; the car slowed, almost stopped, and then proceeded again, slipping down the roadway as the rain bounced high from the surface and black water ran across the tarmac to tumble down over the edge to the slopes below.

Ahead of him, the tail-lights disappeared; seconds later Alan took the bend and saw the car ahead again, braking now as it neared the bend above the reservoir. It was pulling in, lurching over hummocky grass under the wall and Alan considered the position a dangerous one, parking near that bend. If any car came down the hill too fast . . . but then, what fool would be driving too fast on a night like this?

Jeff had been driving too fast. He had slammed straight through the fence, sailing high into the air above the drop to the reservoir . . .

Alan pulled in behind Edwards and cut the engine, then turned off the lights. His hands were shaking; reaction was setting in after the drive up through the valley when he had been able to concentrate on the rain and the windscreen-wipers and push away the words Edwards had used. But not now.

The tapping at the window made him start. He leaned over and unlocked the door. Edwards tumbled into the passenger seat, hair plastered wetly to his forehead, shivering, nervous, like Alan Fearnley. The two men sat there silently for several minutes and outside the rain hammered at the roof of the car as though seeking to get at them.

'Well?' Alan said at last.

Edwards's teeth were chattering. 'This . . . this is where it happened.'

Impatience sharpened Alan's tone. 'For God's sake, I know *that*! But I also know that all the newspaper reports of Jeff's death said it had been an accident. They said . . . they said at the inquest he had been drinking, had returned late from Swansea, and had lost control at the bend.'

'Straight through the fence,' Edwards muttered in a low voice. 'Hell of a crash, you'd have thought. And then an explosion, fire. It made an autopsy difficult.'

'The reports say he had probably been killed instantly.' Alan paused. 'All right, so what are you trying to talk about *murder* for?'

'I've got friends,' Edwards said in a half-whisper.

Alan waited for a few minutes, but when Edwards said no more he grunted. 'The police will have looked into this . . . case. The autopsy will have told them it was an accident. The inquest—'

'One of my friends is in the forensic labs. I seen the report on Jeff Fearnley.'

'And?'

'He died quickly. His skull was crushed, at the front, and also there was a fracture at the back of the head. Splinters of bone—'

'The impact of the crash,' Alan interrupted angrily.

'He wouldn't have known about the fire. He was badly burned, but they think he was already dead—or at least unconscious when the fire took hold. There's that, at least.'

'But you said murder,' Alan said and gripped the driving wheel tightly. 'Was there anything in the forensic report to suggest that? And if so—'

'It was a yellow Porsche,' Edwards interrupted him, almost dreamily. 'You notice me stop up at that lay-by up above? They found some yellow paint up there, as though the Porsche scraped against the wall.'

'You mean he'd lost control as early as that? He hit the rock at the side of the road up there, and then careered on down the hill?'

'That's how the police interpreted it. What about you, Mr Fearnley?'

Alan gritted his teeth. 'I don't know. It's possible.'

'You think so. Me . . . Think about this, Mr Fearnley. You're coming down the road, late at night. You been drinking, but you've now driven maybe thirty miles. So you're tired, too. But nearly home. And the road—you know it well. But you doze, and the liquor makes your eyes funny, affects your eyesight, your co-ordination. And you hit the wall at the side of the road.' Edwards glanced curiously at Alan. 'How do you reckon you'd react, then?'

Alan considered the matter. He was aware of the
dampness of the little man beside him, a faint, musty
odour in his nostrils. 'I . . . I'd try to pull myself together.'

'You hit the wall like that, you get shocked, jumpy,
scared for a few moments. You'd brake maybe, slow.
You'd possibly even stop. But even if you didn't, it's
hardly likely you'd go tearing into the next bend, is it? Or
even if you kept up your speed, on this road you know like
the back of your hand, are you likely to slam straight
through that fence down there?'

'What do the police say to that?'

'For them, it's clear. He was drunk. And a drunk
behind the wheel is a criminal. You know, Mr Fearnley,
my forensic friend tells me they didn't even find any
evidence he'd braked before he hit that bend. Just sailed
straight through. Funny, isn't it?'

Not funny at all. But not sinister, either. Alan was inclined towards the police view. When a man was drunk
behind the wheel of his car, even on a familiar road, his
co-ordination was so poor that anything could happen.
He sat in silence for a little while. At last, Edwards spoke.

'You think it all adds up to nothing, don't you? Just like
the police. But then, that's the comfortable view. The
events are explicable: a drunk goes and kills himself
behind the wheel of a big, flashy Porsche. Shame. And
the fact he was a darts champion — well, hell, everyone
knows they drink like fishes anyway, those boys. So take
the comfortable view. No brake marks in the road . . . so
what? *Suicide*? All right, his darts was going off, but he
was a Catholic, and you can't have suggestions like that
floating around! Too uncomfortable for the family. And
murder? Hell, that's even worse! The police will go for
suspicious circumstances, but they don't go *looking* for
work, do they?'

'You don't sound very convincing to me, Mr Edwards.'

'Hmmm.' Edwards fell silent for a little while. 'All right, but let me put you a different hypothesis. What if your brother was *forced* into that lay-by?'

'I don't understand.'

'A car. Coming up on the outside, going down the hill. It edges him into the side, and he collides with the wall. He stops. The other car stops and someone gets out. And that's when it happens. There's a quarrel, high words. And when Jeff Fearnley turns back to his car he gets it on the back of his head.'

'You can't be serious!'

'There were maybe two men involved—but possibly one. Your brother would have been bundled back into his own car, into the driving seat. The handbrake off, the car trundling down the slope, steered by the man in the passenger seat. A bend, a long run down to the hairpin above the reservoir—and a man leaping out of the passenger seat at the last moment. Dangerous . . . but possible. But that would be why the car didn't swing, didn't brake. It shot straight into the fence, smashed through it, and then took the long dive down to the hill.'

Alan was silent. Edwards sat still beside him, his breath rattling harshly in his chest. The rain hammered on the roof, showing no sign of abatement. Alan shook his head. 'Supposition of this kind . . . where's the proof?'

'Proof? Your brother had alcohol in him all right—but he'd already driven thirty miles. And there's the paint mark at the lay-by—I just don't believe he'd have been reckless enough, however drunk, to go through the fence after a warning scrape at the lay-by. And then there's the double fracture—my friend in the labs, he told me it bothered him, but there was nothing he could report positively. Both injuries *could* have occurred in the car, when it bounced down the slope, with your brother striking his head against the windscreen at first, and then being thrown about, hitting his head again. And the evidence suggests your brother took that front blow on impact. But what if he was *already* unconscious?'

Alan hesitated, turning things over in his mind. He felt edgy, and impatient. He did not know what he was doing with this man up here on the mountain road, but the story he was suggesting was disturbing. He turned slightly in his seat to stare at Edwards. The man was shivering, the wetness of his clothes getting through to him inside the steamy atmosphere of the car. 'All that you say,' Alan suggested quietly, 'equally supports the hypothesis adopted by the police. So what makes you think it went the way you suggest? Surely not the forensic report—the police would have fastened on suspicious circumstances. Your friend—'

'His suspicions were communicated to me only verbally. They're not in the report.'

'Why not?' Alan demanded.

'Because these fellers deal only in *facts!*'

Edwards was immediately aware of the implications of his words. He sat glaring through the windscreen at the slanting rain as Alan took a deep breath. 'All right, Mr Edwards, there it is. Your friend said nothing to the police because he just presents facts, not hypotheses. And that leaves your story in mid-air, doesn't it? Unless you have some other, important fact that throws a different light on things.'

'I have!'

'What is it?'

'It's the company he kept!'

Alan stared at him, puzzled. 'What the hell is that supposed to mean?'

Nick Edwards hunched forward, rocking slightly in the passenger seat. 'Did you ever hear the name Enson?'

'In what context?'

Edwards snorted. 'You name the kind of crooked deal he wasn't involved in! He worked from Swindon in the old days, on the small race meetings, usually over the sticks, and he built up a small business as an on-the-course bookie. In the early seventies he made a good haul — and a legitimate one too, as far as I can discover, by a couple of good bets on his own account. Enough to allow him to branch out, anyway. The trouble is, his branching out was on the darker side of the entertainment.'

'What's that supposed to mean?'

'He'd made a killing on some big races, but he always knew there was more money to be made by rigging races than by taking bets on the course. So he developed a circle of acquaintances with an interesting range of activities. He knew the game on the inside, and he knew how he could put one over on punters and bookies. Off-course betting on long-odds runners, at courses where there was only one line out — and that would be a phone monopolized by one of his cronies at the right time. And then ringers — one horse substituted for another: you'd be surprised how easily it can be done, particularly if the ringer runs under his own registered name, because what's illegal about that?'

Alan was not particularly interested in horse-racing. 'I don't know what you're leading up to.'

'Enson was making a good living, but the fat he wanted was still just beyond reach, so he became more daring, and more careless too. He started strong-arming: if a jockey wouldn't pull a race for him, things could happen to him. It was mainly the amateurs he approached — youngsters out to make a name and hit the big time — and he could scare them off. It got him a two-year stretch at Maidstone. He was out after eight months, on appeal.'

'What was the charge?'

'Grievous bodily harm.' Edwards sniffed. 'On appeal, it was recognized his *personal* involvement was in some doubt and the conviction was therefore overturned. He didn't go back to Swindon after that. In fact, he sort of dropped out. Until three years ago, when he showed up again in Swansea, and using a different name.'

'I don't think I know what—'

Edwards turned his head; his eyes were glittering in the dim light. 'He used to call himself Enson, but the name he uses now is Elias. *Danny Elias!*'

Alan stared at him. Images chased through his mind of the smiling confident man who had come into Aunt Matty's front room and told him about Jeff's prowess at darts; of the excited man who had cheered when Freddy Thomas had won his match at the Black Cat; of the man whose hand had dwelled on Marilyn's shoulder, and whose eyes had been frank and open in their desire. 'Are . . . are you certain of this?'

Edwards's silence was contemptuous: he was certain. Alan remembered where he had first seen the man, at the cemetery on the hillside, watching, observing. But that day, Elias had not been present—he had arrived at the house, later. Then, at the Black Cat, Edwards had been there again—but watching whom, Alan or Elias?

'What do you want with me?' Alan asked, after a short silence.

'I want you to help me, and seek for justice!' Edwards said fiercely.

II

Alan slept badly that night. He did not return to Aunt Matty's house until two in the morning, soaked through; as dawn broke he drifted into a heavy sleep marred with images of violence and pain and when he heard his aunt enter the room it was with difficulty he struggled back to consciousness.

She was standing at the foot of the bed, her sharp little eyes watchful and calculating. 'Your clothes are soaked,' she said accusingly. 'I'll get them dried. What's the matter?'

There was no possible way in which he could tell her. Indeed, quite apart from the distress it would cause her, what was there to tell? When she called him downstairs, some twenty minutes later, he ate the large fried breakfast she had made for him and said little, churning over in his mind the story Edwards had told him, and his own uncertainties increased as the morning wore on. It was not merely that the events surrounding Jeff's death, the way Edwards recounted them, were hard to believe, there was also the motivation behind Edwards's own actions — his seeking for justice. An odd way to put it: it suggested a crusading zeal, yet at the same time it held personal undercurrents that made it suspect to Alan Fearnley.

He was standing in the front room, staring at Jeff's trophies, still proudly displayed by his aunt, when he heard the ringing of the phone. A few seconds later Aunt Matty called out to him. Alan walked into the sitting-room and took the receiver from her. She made no attempt to leave the room, but sat down in an easy chair, watching him.

'Hello? This is Alan Fearnley.'

'*Alan*!' There was exasperation in the tone at the other end of the line. 'About time! I've had one hell of a job finding out where you are!'

It was Peter Emburey, senior executive in Emburey Associates, and the last man Alan wanted to speak to at this particular time. Alan hesitated. 'Hello, Peter. I . . . I'm sorry. I needed to take a few days off — '

'Right. They told me — *eventually*. Your brother's death. I'm sorry about that — but you hadn't seen him in years, had you?'

Alan's glance flickered involuntarily towards Aunt Matty. Her flint eyes made him feel she could hear what Emburey had said. 'I needed time to sort a few things out here.'

'I understand that. But what's the deal, not telling us where you were? I had to screw it out of your secretary that she *thought* you'd gone to Wales, and then all kinds of bloody detective work was necessary to run you to earth at your aunt's place. Even then, it was just that Diana . . .' There was a brief pause, a hesitation that dried Alan's mouth. Peter Emburey rushed on. 'Anyway, look here, the fact is, things are moving and I need to get a few things straight. When'll you be back at Bristol?'

'I . . . I'm not sure.'

'Not *sure*? Hell's flames, Alan . . . Have you seen Stevenson yet?'

'I've seen him. He asked some rather . . . rather awkward questions.'

'But nothing you couldn't handle, right? The thing is, we need those audited accounts as soon as possible. Have you processed them yet? Got them there with you?'

'No, I'm afraid not.'

There was a short silence. 'Alan, you know I'm relying on you in this. Those figures—pressures are building up and—'

'Peter, I'm sorry,' Alan cut in suddenly. 'I can't speak now. I'll be in touch.'

Abruptly he put the phone down. He looked up and Aunt Matty was staring at him hungrily, leaning forward slightly in her chair. It was as though he were a boy again, caught out in some misdemeanour and about to be subjected to the kind of interrogation that would leave him squirming, guilty, confessional, even if the guilt was minimal and the fault not his. Aunt Matty had always had that capacity, to unravel his mind and his strength, and he guessed now it had been a need in her, an inexplicable urge to dominate, something she would probably deny and not even understand herself.

'There's trouble,' she said.

'No. Just business,' he said flatly.

'I know you, Alan. Something's bothering you. Tell me.'

'There's nothing to tell.'

'There is. It's burdening you. I've seen it ever since you came back. I've wondered whether it was Jeff's funeral that brought you back, even; it could be something else, the thing that's on your mind.'

'I've told you. Just business.'

'No.'

She wanted to say she could help, if only he would throw back the barriers he had erected in his flight from her and the valley, but she had changed over the years too, and some of the fire had gone, damped down by a reluctance to expose herself to her nephew. It would be a reluctance based upon a growing insecurity, as age touched her and her world changed. For a moment Alan wanted to reach out to her, explain, but the knowledge that it would be an indulgence, a seeking for support when his problems were his own, to be dealt with personally, stopped him. He might *need* help and support, but he must not seek it, for it would be a sign of weakness. Ruefully, he admitted to himself that he was as firmly rooted in his stubbornness as she was in her desire to dominate.

And yet he needed to talk. Not about Diana and his tottering marriage; not about Emburey Associates and the decisions he had to take in their regard. He had to talk to someone about the rain on the mountain road, and about Nick Edwards, and the wild things the little man had had to say in the darkness where Jeff had died. It could not be Aunt Matty. There was only one other person he could turn to.

The phone rang insistently while Alan and Aunt Matty sat silently, facing each other: Peter Emburey, furious at having been cut off, would be trying to reach Alan again.

A gesture stopped Aunt Matty picking up the phone; they sat there quietly, looking at each other, aunt and nephew, and finally, when the phone fell silent, Alan stood up.

'I'm going out for a while, now. I don't think I'll be back for lunch.'

She made no reply, but her face was stiff and her eyes hostile.

Alan used the public call-box in the village to phone Marilyn, but it was Jim Carter who answered. The warning pips sounded and Alan hung up. He walked into the park and sat on a bench: a group of lads were playing touch rugby on the grass and the sun gleamed fitfully from behind intermittent cloud, but the rains of the night before still glistened on the hillside and he was unable to escape the words that still moved in his brain.

An hour later he rang again. This time Marilyn answered.

'Was that you ringing a while back?' she asked conspiratorially.

'Yes. I want to see you. To talk.'

'It sounds urgent. Are . . . are you all right?'

'Fine. Where can we meet? And when?'

Their previous meeting had been sharpened by its clandestine nature. So was this one, but the edge was different: Marilyn had known from the tone of his voice that something was bothering him, and it would not be their relationship. Their meeting-place, they had decided, would not be a café, or an hotel: instead, they each drove to a pre-arranged rendezvous at the top of the valley, where ancient quarrying had hollowed out an area where they could park off the road, and more recent local government philanthropy had established wooden seats from which they could command a view of the valley floor, twisting, black-rivered, for three miles below them, the terraces climbing and clinging to the steep-sided slopes still scarred by greening coal-tips.

When she came to join him on the seat, in the hazy sunshine, he pointed to the evidence of past industry. 'I wonder how long it'll take them to disappear into the hillside?'

'The tips?' She shrugged. 'After our time, I expect. Unless they tumble into the valley itself—and with rain like last night, that's always possible, around here.' She paused, eyeing him carefully. 'You got back all right, after leaving me in Cardiff?'

'More or less.'

'What's that supposed to mean? What happened?'

He hesitated. 'I . . . I had a talk to someone. I'll tell you about it shortly, but first . . . were you at Swansea, the night Jeff died?'

Her eyes widened slightly, and she shook her head. 'No. I can take just so many darts matches. I gave that one a miss. Besides, since it was Swansea, I thought it politic not to go.'

'I don't understand.'

There was a trace of bitterness in her laugh. 'Let's put it like this. When you're married a while, and things begin to go wrong, there are certain signals you begin to recognize. Some of them came to me clearly enough. An extra care, when a husband dresses. Late returns at night . . . and sometimes no returns at all. Especially from particular locations—or places within striking distance of certain towns. And then, confirmations.'

'How do you mean?'

She shrugged. 'The odd word . . . gossip . . . glances and grins between men. A woman recognizes the signs. And others. Like taking a bath.' She smiled, and shook her head. 'I'll say that about Jim—where other men might take a bath *before* they visit another woman, he always took one afterwards, before he came back to my bed. There's consideration, isn't it?' She gave him a sidelong glance. 'And he usually took a bath after return-ing from Swansea—as he did that night, even though he got in about three in the morning. *Very* considerate.'

'So you didn't go because you knew Jim was probably going to see someone.'

'That's about the size of it. But why do you want to know?'

'I don't. All I want to know is what happened that night. You'll all have talked about it, even if you weren't there on that evening. What have you heard, Marilyn?'

She frowned, puzzled. 'Heard? About what? The match, you mean?' She looked around her at the moun-tain, and the valley, as though seeking clarity of recall in the scenery about her. 'It wasn't a good night for Jeff, I know. That's probably why he sank so many pints.'

'Tell me about it.'

'Well, he was off form, I suppose—that's the beginning and end of it. I'd seen him at a match the previous week, and though I don't know too much about the game's finer points, I got the impression he'd lost his skill . . . though they'll tell you that doesn't happen. It's just the concentration. Whatever the right of it, Jeff certainly wasn't the world beater he'd been, and in a way, what I'd seen earlier was confirmed that night.'

'He had a bad night?'

'He had a *lucky* night. From the way I've heard it, his form was poor, but first one of his main rivals was taken sick, another didn't turn up because of a breakdown on the M6, and when he faced Freddy, well, he was just plain lucky. Freddy's arrows kept hitting the wire, his early darts blocked some of the beds, he just wasn't getting his doubles, and Jeff pulled off some flukey shots which gave him what he needed at the crucial times.'

'So Jeff won?'

'That's right. And the crowd didn't like it.' She paused

reflectively. 'You might have got the wrong impression the other evening: they're not just a wild, crazy-shouting lot. They know the game, appreciate the skills and the finer points — and they enjoy the rivalry and the edge that exists between the better players. And most of all they like a winner.'

'Which is why Jeff was popular?' Alan asked.

'That's right. But it's not just a matter of winning. It's the *way* you win, as well. And that night Jeff didn't win well. He was in the final against Freddy and he wasn't playing well. Freddy should have taken him, walked through the match. But the luck ran against him, and in spite of Jeff's poor form, he made it yet again.'

'It didn't please the crowd?'

'That's an understatement.' Marilyn pulled a face. 'From all accounts, they just about howled Jeff off the stage.'

Alan considered the matter for a short while. 'Was that why Jeff drank heavily that night?'

She waved a doubtful hand and shook her head. 'Jeff always sank a fair few . . . No, he'd been drinking pretty heavily before that, all week as a matter of fact. Not a *lot* more than usual, but enough for some of us to notice. But being off form, maybe he was down in the dumps. They all regard themselves as *artists*, you know,' she added, with a wry smile, 'and treat themselves to bouts of depression if their art isn't working.'

'It's likely, nevertheless, that Jeff drank pretty heavily that night because he'd won so badly, and because his form was poor?'

'That's the general idea.'

'What happened then?'

Marilyn shrugged. 'It followed the usual pattern for Swansea nights, it seems. When the match was over, Jim slipped away to go visit his little piece in Neath. Freddy and Jeff and the others, they stayed on and did their socializing bit. At about eleven, Jeff went out to his Porsche and drove home. And that was that. The irony is, after thirty miles, it was the last few that killed him. But that's the way things go, I suppose.'

'When did you hear about the . . . the accident?'

She teased at her lower lip with a finger in an oddly childlike gesture. 'It would be about ten in the morning, I think. Jim was still in bed in the spare room.' She glanced at Alan sardonically. 'Not only a bath, but also the desire not to disturb me when he got back *really* late. Anyway, the police called, got Jim up, and off they went. By the time he came back, it was all over the village anyway that Jeff had been killed. Jim was pretty shaken . . .'

Alan hesitated. 'When did Danny Elias appear on the scene?'

She stared at him in surprise. 'At the time of the accident, you mean?'

'No, no . . . when did he get to know Jeff, that sort of thing?'

She frowned, obviously puzzled by the sudden switch in Alan's questions. 'Let me think . . . I suppose it would be about three, maybe four years ago. Jeff had begun to make a name for himself in the clubs and won a few competitions, and he, Freddy and Jim had formed an exhibition team. I think Danny Elias first met them in a club in Bridgend, suggested a match in a club he had an interest in, Swansea way. That's how it started. After that, he arranged the odd match night, but once Jeff turned pro, and he and Freddy left the factory, Danny kind of faded out a bit. Jim stepped back to organize their programme, and Danny stayed friendly, kept an interest, like, but didn't get involved too much. Not really his major interest, you see.'

'What is?'

'Apart from women, you mean?' She grinned at him wickedly. 'I've had to give him the push a couple of times when he got too amorous, I'll tell you! No, his main interests lie in his clubs — he's got a stake in a couple in Swansea, and his betting shops. He spends a fair bit of time at the races from Chester northwards, and he follows the dogs, particularly on the Cardiff track.'

'His main interest is still betting, then. And I gather he often places bets on the darts matches.'

She stared at him, frowning. 'A lot of people do. Look, Alan, I think I've been pretty patient. What's this all about? You sounded a bit odd over the phone, I guessed something was disturbing you, but all I've had from you so far is a series of questions, unconnected as far as I can see. What's happened? And why the sudden interest in Danny Elias?'

Alan hesitated. He stared across the valley to the slopes opposite, green and brown, dotted with tiny white specks, sheep grazing on the free hills. He remembered dustbins overturned in back lanes by foraging sheep, when they had still been given the freedom of the streets. Things were different now; everything changed. But not so suddenly, and forcibly, as last night.

'Danny Elias isn't his real name, I'm told,' he said at last. 'Originally he was called Enson.'

'So?'

'He served a period in prison after attacks on some jockey or other. He always did have an interest in the turf, and in making money, it seems. And when he came out, he changed his name and moved back to Wales — where from his accent it would seem he originated.'

'He's from Porthcawl, in the first place.' Her eyes searched his features, seeking answers to unspoken questions.

'I learned this from a man I met last night. I'd seen him before — at the cemetery, and at the Black Cat. He . . . he took me up the Bwlch-y-Clawdd, after you and I parted last night.'

'You were up there in the rain?'

'That's right. You see . . .' The pause stretched, lengthened, as he found difficulty getting out the words. It was all so unbelievable, so difficult to comprehend; it could only be some sick fantasy, some obsession, and yet now the seeds of suspicion had been sown in his mind they were growing, expanding into a festering anxiety that needed balm. 'This man . . . he's called Edwards. He . . . he's of the opinion that Jeff's death was not an accident.'

He heard the sharp intake of breath but he did not look at her. She said nothing for several minutes; they sat side by side on the wooden bench, staring out over the valley. When he rose, abruptly, she rose with him: they both felt the need to walk, to think, to churn over the facts they knew and had accepted.

After a while, in a small, tight voice, she said, 'I just can't credit this, Alan. Are you suggesting Jeff was . . . was *murdered?*'

'I'm not suggesting it. This man Edwards . . .' He went on briefly and hurriedly, to explain to her just what Nick Edwards had told him the previous night. When he had finished she shook her head.

'But why should anyone want to kill Jeff? And who?'

Alan hesitated. 'Edwards has ideas about that, though they're only half formed. They involve Danny Elias.'

'*Danny?*' She stopped and stared at him. 'That's why you were asking the questions about Danny earlier! You can't be serious, Alan!'

Alan shrugged. 'I don't know whether I am or not. This man Edwards is certainly serious. He's got no *proof*, but he's got a theory that in some way Jeff will have crossed Elias, that maybe there was a quarrel at Swansea, and that Elias followed Jeff, caught up with him on the mountain and killed him.'

'But *why*, for God's sake?'

Alan stared about him at the mountain slopes, frown-

ing. 'Edwards thinks it will be something to do with the
betting on Jeff. He's convinced, as he puts it, that once a
race-rigger, always a race-rigger. He thinks Danny is one
kind of leopard that will never change his spots, and he
puts his back record of cheating on the race-track and
physical violence off it against what he sees as suspicious
circumstances surrounding Jeff's death.'

'Neither the police . . . nor anyone else has seen anything suspicious about it.'

'Until Edwards raises the doubts,' Alan said. 'Then . . .'
He looked at her and saw uncertainties stain her eyes. 'On
the other hand, there's something about Edwards himself
that isn't . . . well, quite right.'

'How do you mean?'

Alan turned, started to walk again, head lowered in
thought, and Marilyn kept pace with him, close to his
elbow. 'This man Edwards, he told me a little of his own
background. It ties in, to some extent, with Danny
Elias—or Enson, as Edwards calls him. It seems Edwards
was a newspaperman, working on one of the Cardiff evening papers and then took a job with a provincial paper on
the south coast. He got married there, and had a small
child, then finally picked up a job with a London paper,
one of the tabloids who like to produce their news in as
lurid a manner as possible. Edwards got hold of the Enson
story pretty early on, and from what he says, did two
years' investigative reporting on Enson before it all blew
up. Enson got put away, only to be released again shortly
afterwards, on appeal. In the meanwhile, things happened to Nick Edwards.'

'What sort of things?'

'He received several warnings from the London area:
he couldn't pinpoint the source, because he was reporting
not only the race-track gangs, but also some of the
shadier sides of London life. Then his young son got
knocked down in the street in a hit-and-run accident, and

while Enson was in prison there were several threatening phone calls made to his home, when his wife was there alone. It was too much for her: she took an overdose of sleeping pills, and died.'

'How horrible!'

Alan nodded. 'Edwards himself then started to slide, it seems. When Enson came out of prison, Edwards was already hitting the bottle hard. In the end, it cost him his job, and though he tried the provincials again, he was regarded as unreliable. And . . . well, that's why his whole story worries me.'

'Because he has been . . . or is . . . a drunk?'

Alan shook his head. 'I don't think he is on the bottle now. No, what worries me is his *intensity*. I'm sure he can't know who sent him threatening letters — he certainly doesn't know who knocked down his son. But he *feels* he knows who is responsible — and all the hurt, and the pain, loss and humiliation he's suffered over the last few years tend to crystallize, head him in one direction.'

Marilyn stared at him. 'Danny Elias?'

Alan nodded. 'I think he's obsessed with Elias. I'm sure he sees him as the author of all his ills. He hasn't said so, but I think, whether he admits it to himself or not, he's driven to a pursuit of Elias because he feels the man is in some way responsible — either directly or indirectly, for the death of his son and his wife, and his own personal troubles. He put Elias in prison once — for it was partly his evidence that secured a conviction — and he wants to do it again. It's a crusade, if you like —'

'And Jeff's death will be the means? That makes it all highly suspect, Alan.'

'I know. That's why I had to talk to someone — to you — about it. I wasn't around when Jeff died; I didn't know him any more; I knew little or nothing of the life he led, the kind of person he was; and I knew nothing of his friends, the circle in which he moved. Edwards seems to know a great deal about the darker side of the sporting world. Who am I to say that he's wrong in suspecting Jeff was murdered? And he claims to know Elias — or Enson — from years back. Should I merely discount what he says? I *feel* I should, when cold common sense and logic point to the fact that the police have no suspicions; and when I recognize the obsessional signs in the man's voice and face, I become even more positive. But then . . . what if there's something in what he says? What if he's *right*?'

'Danny always bet on Jeff,' Marilyn said quietly. 'He would have had no reason to kill him; as far as I know they were friendly.'

'Edwards thinks it might have had something to do with Elias's betting circles,' Alan insisted.

Marilyn was silent for a little while as they walked slowly along above the road that snaked to the top of the hill. At last she nodded. 'I think there's someone you ought to have a word with.' She glanced at him, a furrow of concern on her brow. 'He's called Ned Turtle: you'll find him at the New Inn tonight.'

III

The long room was crowded and its atmosphere stained with cigarette smoke. The walls were dark-panelled, brown, and decorated with faded photographs of rugby teams from the 1920s, sporting prints of long-forgotten racehorses, and occasional fresh-faced, stern-visaged young boxers who would have held a brief valley fame before venturing into the wider, professional world outside and a quick oblivion. The bar itself ran the length of the room, its scars unpolished, its dark wood heavily stained, but the brass foot-rest, though dented and misshapen, gleamed brightly in the dim light. It was a male room, and a dated room: Alan felt as though the men here found a comfort that they would have lost outside in the changing face of the valley. In the New Inn nothing changed except the faces; its timelessness, frozen by an insistent resistance to change that would be emotional as much as practical, was the centre of a world for the men who patronized it. Alan's uncle had come here for years, for the statutory half-pints allowed by Aunt Matty. Now there were younger, harder-drinking men present — but no women.

Ned Turtle sat in a corner. He was a small, bald, round man with gentle eyes and a soft, downturned mouth. He was dressed in a shabby suit that, according to Marilyn, belied his financial status, for as one of the most successful turf accountants in the valley he would have a considerable bank balance to support him in his old age. Indeed, it was his money which indirectly had given rise to his name: some years ago he had been 'turned over' by some young roughs, out to steal what money he had in the house, and he had lain on his back, pleading with them to leave him alone with his slipped disc. They had, empty-handed, and Ned had never identified them thereafter — through philanthropy or fear no one was sure, but ever after he was known as Ned Turtle.

He drank whisky and water and he eyed the glass Alan brought him with the occupational suspicion of a bookmaker accepting a doubtful bet.

'My name's Alan Fearnley.'

Ned Turtle's brown eyes narrowed; his glance moved over Alan's features, testing, questioning. 'Don't look much like your brother.'

'Did you know him well?'

'Saw him play, often enough. As an arrow man, one of the greatest. Could always see *him* off.'

There was a veiled contempt in his tone as his glance

flickered across the room to the knot of men near the window, and the darts board mounted on the far wall. Alan looked across: he had not noticed Freddy Thomas when he came in, but he saw the man now, sitting quietly on a bench under the window, watching the game being played in front of him.

'That mattered to Freddy,' Alan said, almost to himself.

'It mattered all right. He *bled* every time Jeff Fearnley took him — and that was for two, three years. Aye, it mattered.' Ned Turtle reached carefully for the drink Alan had brought him. 'You ever see your brother play?'

'No.'

'Ah, man, when he was on song . . .'

'I gather, just before he . . . he died, his form wasn't so good.'

Ned Turtle sipped noisily at his drink. He seemed to regard the noise as an expression of his satisfaction with the gift. He replaced the glass on the table, and replied, 'I hear that was the way of it — though he still beat Freddy up at Swansea. But I was never all that interested in the game. The dogs is my passion, and the horses my living.'

'So you didn't do much business on darts?'

Ned Turtle looked at him blandly. 'Didn't say that, boy. Take a bet on anything, I will. But darts wasn't *big* business for me, ever. Just a sideline, though there was occasional flurries, like, when the big matches was on and a local boy like Jeff was involved. Plenty of punters around then.'

'What about Danny Elias? Did he have heavy bets on darts matches?'

The turf accountant reached for his glass, not so much because he wanted a drink, but rather to give himself time to consider an answer. Carefully he said, 'He'd flutter a bit — but then, he's got his own string of shops. You'd be better off asking him.'

'I thought . . . I've heard I might get a straighter answer from *you*.'

'Now what would make you think that, boy?'

Something glinted deep in the soft brown eyes but the downturned mouth seemed more lugubrious than ever. Alan inspected his own glass of lager. 'Well,' he said quietly, 'the way I hear it there's no love lost between you and Danny Elias, and you're also one of the fraternity who keep their ears to the ground, professionally speaking. You know most of what goes on in the betting world.'

'That's so.' The complacency in his tone was not matched by the watchfulness in his eyes. 'I learned the hard way — you got to know what's going on, all the time.'

Marilyn had already told Alan about Ned Turtle's involvement with Elias. She had not known the full story, but it seemed Elias had taken some large bets and, as was the practice, he had begun to lay them off with other bookmakers. So far, there could be no complaint, but it was said that Elias had then used a group of punters at a race in Chester to place bets systematically in each of Ned's shops, at a given time, just three minutes before the start of the race. The bets had been on an outsider; the shops had had no time to check with each other; within three minutes five thousand pounds had been laid and the horse came in at three to one. Elias had used Ned Turtle not to lay off bets but to place his own and make a killing. Ned Turtle had no reason to love Danny Elias.

'I just wondered,' Alan said, 'whether you'd heard anything about the betting on my brother during the Swansea championship.'

'A few items came my way,' Ned Turtle said, and finished his whisky. 'Ahhh . . . there'll be trouble, soon.'

He was looking past Alan to the darts board and the group under the window. A young red-haired man was standing in front of Freddy Thomas in heated discussion. It seemed that the young man was challenging Thomas but Freddy Thomas considered, sneeringly, that the stakes were too low to bother.

'All right!' the youngster shouted. 'I'll make it sixty quid, against three legs!'

Freddy Thomas's quiet, contemptuous reply was too low for Alan to hear and he turned back; Ned Turtle was smiling coldly. He shook his head. 'There's always some young gunfighter who thinks he can do it. That silly young bugger will end up this evening with a hole in his pocket and a bigger one in his pride. Freddy'll take him for every penny he's got—and humiliate him into the bargain. A cold bastard, Freddy. That's where he was like your brother—and different from him too.'

'I don't understand.'

'Jeff Fearnley had to put up with this kind of thing all the time—he was always a target for the young chancers who'd want to be able to boast they had out-shot the great Jeff Fearnley. But he had a way of discouraging them: first, he'd up the stake-money into the hundreds, so they'd back off; if they didn't, he'd suggest the match should take place on a stage before an invited audience—so everyone could see how good the youngster was. That was usually enough. But Freddy . . . he's not like that. I know what'll happen now—he'll push that carrot-head up to his limit, maybe a hundred—but not to make him back off. Just to nail him, make him look small. Aye . . . there he goes.'

Alan looked back. Thomas was rising, darts in hand. The cocky red-head was stepping back, grinning, but pale-faced now he had succeeded in bringing Thomas forward to the challenge. 'Bloody fool,' Ned Turtle snorted. 'Drink?'

Alan insisted on getting the bookmaker another. When he returned to Ned Turtle's table the crowd around the darts board had increased, and from the laughter and noise it seemed Freddy Thomas was already about to take the first leg, with a minimum of effort.

'He'll whitewash him,' Ned Turtle said in prescient satisfaction and sipped at his whisky.

'We were talking about Elias, and the Swansea match,' Alan reminded him.

'Aye, we were.' The brown eyes were still gentle, but there was a spark of malice in their depths. 'Funny, it was, that week. He worked . . . uncharacteristically, you might say.'

'Elias?'

'Aye. Lost a fair bit that night.'

'You mean he bet *against* Jeff?'

'That's about the size of it. Funny, that. You see, Danny Elias is a *real* gambler. Plays percentages. Knows his winners, and gets his money on them — never mind the odds. No good backing long shots if they don't come in. So the odds were short, always, on Jeff: if he kept winning, you had to bet on him. And Danny Elias was always a supporter of your brother, as far as bets went. But that night, things were different. He had money . . . a lot of money riding on Freddy Thomas. And Freddy blew it.' He lifted his glass and inspected it casually. 'Or, of course, Jeff did.'

Alan stared at him, puzzled. 'Jeff *won* the match.'

'That's right,' Ned Turtle replied, and sipped at his whisky, savouring its taste.

For a few moments Alan was unable to understand what Ned Turtle was suggesting. Then, frowning, he leaned forward. 'Are you suggesting Jeff had some kind of . . . arrangement with Elias, and then didn't follow it through?'

Ned Turtle's eyes were sad. 'Don't get me wrong, boy. I'm not *suggesting* anything. I'm simply giving you a few facts, of the kind you been asking for. Look, Danny Elias always bets on certs. He's backed Jeff often. Suddenly, that week, from all accounts Jeff was a bit off form. But he was still the big man, the man to beat. So there was talk that maybe Freddy could take him — still only talk, because Jeff Fearnley had a kind of hoodoo on that boy over there. Now then, what happens? Two blokes don't appear that night — so a Freddy-Jeff final is on. Coincidence? I don't know. Then, in that final, Jeff is odds-on favourite — but from what I hear, Danny Elias made a bad mistake. He put a pile of money on *Freddy*. Who blew it.'

'That wasn't what you were suggesting.'

'Hold on. There's an *alternative* possibility.'

'That Elias had an arrangement with Jeff,' Alan said reluctantly, 'that he should play badly, and lose to Thomas. Elias would pick up a lot of money — and maybe Jeff would be sharing in it.'

'Your words boy, not mine,' Ned Turtle said complacently. 'But I've known funnier stories. With just as funny endings. Things can always go wrong, where money's involved. This case now, it could be that Freddy was in on it too. Maybe it was him that blew it — story is, his luck was bloody awful that night. Or Jeff Fearnley had the luck of the devil. But you know, a *good* player, a *really* good player, can hit the wire when he wants to, can make darts bounce out when he needs to, can con everyone that he's off form, and then charge through, seemingly lucky as hell, to take the prize. I've seen Freddy Thomas do it, playing with a chancer like that one . . . Hah, there he goes, down the drain, see?' There was a roar of laughter and clapping from the other side of the room. 'Freddy's nailed him on the second leg, clean as a whistle. That's carrot-head's money and temper gone . . . But I was saying, a good player can do these things. Question is: who was playing the con that night, if there was one? Freddy or Jeff? And which of them — if anyone at all, sold Danny Elias down the river? Intriguin', isn't it?'

'What you've told me —'

'Supposition, boy, guesses. There's talk, of course, but it's rubber talk—bounces around, never still. Unreliable. Like people. But I got to go now—missus'll be expecting me. Nice to meet you, Mr Fearnley, and thanks for the drinks.'

He hoisted himself to his feet, nodded, and made his way to the doors. Alan watched him go, and then looked across the room to the darts group. The game was over, the red-haired youngster drowning his humiliation in a pint of bitter. Freddy Thomas was standing, with a half-pint in his hand. He was staring at Alan Fearnley.

Their glances locked for a long moment, then Freddy Thomas turned aside, said something to his companions. He finished his glass, placed it on the table, then walked across to where Alan was sitting.

' 'Evening,' he said quietly. 'Surprised to see you here.'

Alan looked up. He did not like Freddy Thomas. He was not sure why he disliked him: it might have been the man's cold, level commitment; it might have been his manner. Or there might have been other reasons, half-formed impressions he had not yet identified and clarified.

'Not exactly your scene, like,' Thomas added.

'I just felt like a drink.'

'With Ned Turtle? Funny company.'

There was a controlled belligerance in the man, but its base was uneasiness. Alan stared at him, watched the narrowed eyes, the thin line of the mouth, and at last, casually, he said, 'I came in to see him, in fact. Wanted a chat with him.'

'Like I said, bookies is funny company for a man like you.'

'I wanted to talk to him about the Swansea match.'

Something sagged momentarily in Freddy Thomas's face: it was as though he found himself face to face with his own humiliation. Perhaps there were echoes of his own treatment of the red-haired youngster drinking in the corner; perhaps it was something deeper and more fundamental—the knowledge of his own inferiority whenever he had faced Jeff Fearnley. He dragged a chair forward, sat down abruptly. 'The Swansea match? Me and Jeff, you mean?'

'That's right. I was . . . interested.'

'In what?'

'In the way it went.'

Freddy Thomas grimaced, baring his teeth wolfishly. He looked away from Alan, across the room to his defeated challenger as though seeking some measure of confidence and approval. He ran the back of his hand across his mouth in a nervous, irritable gesture. 'He was mine that night. I could have taken him.'

'But you didn't.'

Thomas glared at Alan. There were pale flecks of anger in his eyes, but there was something else too, a buried uncertainty that must have always been there, whenever he had faced Jeff Fearnley. 'It was just . . . bad luck. It was *my* night. But everything went wrong. Jeff was placed under no pressure early on—two withdrawals. And when we fought it out, I had him, several times—and each time something went wrong. I *knew* I could take him that night. But he was lucky . . .'

And yet as he stared at Thomas's anxious, earnest features Alan knew that there had been more than luck to it. Skill could overcome bad luck: the fact was, Thomas had never really *believed* he could beat Jeff Fearnley. And that lack of belief had destroyed his game. He had not been able to maintain his skills under the pressure of his own lack of confidence.

'I understand Danny Elias had a lot of money riding on you that night.'

Freddy Thomas blinked. 'I don't pay attention to fellers who back me. I play for other reasons.'

'The story is, Elias lost a fair bit, when Jeff came through. You didn't know?'

Sulkily Thomas muttered, 'I heard something about it.'

'There's also a rumour . . .' Alan began, but he never finished the sentence. Thomas was looking at him, and there was something in his expression that killed the words on Alan's lips. He had seen the commitment in Freddy Thomas at the Black Cat; he had seen the cold-ness with which he had first needled the red-haired youngster and then destroyed him in his challenge match; now, he felt for the first time that Thomas's cold commit-ment was characteristic. It was not confined merely to the game at which he excelled: he felt the same way about life. He had to win, at any cost — and a man who felt that way about life could be dangerous. There were undercur-rents of violence in Freddy Thomas, and they seethed, explosively, at no great distance beneath the surface.

The thought remained with Alan when he went to bed that night; the thought, and the words that Ned Turtle had spoken to him.

'*Question is: who was playing the con that night, if there was one? Freddy or Jeff? And which of them — if anyone at all, sold Danny Elias down the river?*'

One of them — Jeff — was dead.

CHAPTER 4

I

In the overcast afternoon heavy dark clouds built up in the east and flickers of pale lightning sent distant brief glows to menace the gloomy horizon. The narrow, hedged roads above Caerphilly were silent; no birds sang. The hawthorn was still and lifeless, there was no movement in the heavy air and the world seemed expectant, waiting for something to happen, and the green of the fields was dull under the grey, stolid sky.

Outside Newport the traffic became congested and Alan's shirt was damp, sticking to his back as he drove. It had been an odd, puzzling morning.

It had begun with a visit from Nick Edwards. The little ex-newspaperman had been eager to hear what had transpired since he had first spoken to Alan, but Alan's uneasiness had grown when he saw the sharp obsessive need in the man's face. Edwards wanted information — but *any* information would do to fuel his own peculiar view of the situation. He had an inner conviction that would be bolstered by any chance remark, and no matter how threadlike the evidence he would twist and weave it into a rope to support his personal theories.

'But what else could you infer from what this bookmaker Ned Turtle was trying to tell you?' Edwards had demanded. His eyes were bright, almost feverish in their excitement. 'It's perfectly obvious, surely! Something happened between your brother and Danny Elias. Ned Turtle maintains that Elias always bet on Jeff Fearnley. Suddenly, that week, he doesn't — and Jeff Fearnley is off form. It's all so obvious!'

'Not to me,' Alan had demurred.

'I hesitate to say it — even though I didn't know your brother — but the facts are so . . . *convincing*. They *must* have had some deal arranged! But Jeff couldn't go through with it. Because of the factor Elias hadn't taken into account.'

'And what was that?'

Edwards's narrow face had been alight with subdued excitement, his eyes dancing, blazing with an inner conviction. 'Oh, hell, it's nothing new! I've seen it time and again in the world I've moved in. You see, the average sportsman plays for fun, but your *professional*, he's different. There's something else, something inexplicable in human terms, maybe something to do with human perfection, that drives him on. It doesn't really matter how his particular sport is regarded, or what the accolades might be. In a sense, they're unimportant. They are the external badges he wins, and seeks — but there's something a damn sight more important to him. It's what he thinks of himself: a matter of pride.'

'I'm not sure I understand.'

'If you'd lived close to the sporting world, you would. Think of it. There's money beginning to pour into the darts matches — television, big business, sponsorship. Your brother was beginning to be rated a phenomenon, and there was money in that. But *entertainment* demands *challenge*. You know what I would have said to Jeff Fearnley, had I been Danny Elias? And remember, I *know* that man: I'm inside his skin.'

'All right, tell me.'

Nick Edwards's eyes glowed. 'I'd have said — Cash in, boy, and do yourself a bit of good. Show that you're *vulnerable* — because two things will come out of that. First of all, since they all think you're unbeatable we could make a packet if you got beaten, surprisingly, by the one man you've consistently hammered — Freddy Thomas. Then, afterwards, the entertainment value rises as the uncertainty appears — can Thomas take you again? The sponsorship side will go up, the public interest will rise. It's worth it, I would have said to Jeff Fearnley. You throw this match, I'll put a few thousand on Thomas as a side bet, you'll collect a percentage — and next time, you can really show Thomas, and the public, who's the champion.'

'But that's not the way it happened.'

'Precisely. It's what I'm trying to say. Sportsmen are funny people. They can take that kind of decision — racing, football, boxing, darts — they're all the same. There's an element of corruption in them all, as soon as money plays its part, as soon as gambling becomes an integral part of the sport. But there's the one element you can never rely on: the individual, and his sense of pride.'

'You mean Jeff might have changed his mind?'

'Not even that. I think he and Elias had a deal going: Jeff would throw the Swansea match for an immediate return, in terms of cash, and bigger purses thereafter once he was seen to be vulnerable. And Jeff was going through with it — until he and Freddy were in front of that board, with that crowd howling behind them. And then it would be something Jeff wouldn't have been able to control. No matter what deal he'd entered into, his own pride of performance, his own *need* to demonstrate his skills, the necessity he must have felt to show he would always be better than Freddy Thomas — all this would have meant he wouldn't have been able to go through with his arrangement with Elias. And he put Thomas down again — even though he stood to lose money by it.'

'I'm not sure —'

'But think of what Ned Turtle said! And then think about what must have happened on the Bwlch-y-Clawdd.'

Nick Edwards had spelled it out. If Jeff Fearnley had indeed welshed on his arrangement with Danny Elias, the ex-race-rigger would have had every reason to be angry. Jeff had stayed on at the Swansea club, drinking hard, probably aware that his own pride had led him into a situation of some danger; Elias himself would have wanted a confrontation, an explanation that would have been impossible to obtain in the crowded night-club.

So it had been the mountain road. Jeff had left in the Porsche: Elias, with a henchman, or possibly alone, had driven after him, and above the lay-by had forced him into the side. An angry discussion, an altercation, a violent reaction.

And then it was done.

'It's the way it *was*,' Edwards had insisted. 'Can't you see it? Maybe it was Elias personally; maybe it wasn't. It could have been some of his cronies, out to exact a physical payment from Jeff. It makes no difference. I tell you it all fits: Elias put your brother over that edge, and killed him. All we need is the final proofs—the circumstances are all there.'

But it was like the sky now, in the afternoon: heavy thunderclouds and intermittent, dangerous gleams in the dark clouds. Nick Edwards's obsessional hatred for Elias could darken his judgement, and the lightning flashes of hate flickered through as warnings to Alan Fearnley. He had left Nick Edwards, still unconvinced, but disturbed, and he had gone on to keep his appointment with the bank manager, Mr Lloyd.

The rotund, barrel-chested, balding bank manager had been at his most pompous and prim. Alan Fearnley had, on the occasion of his first visit, called his professional competence into question. He was not the man to make light of his present knowledge.

'Ah, Mr Fearnley, I'm pleased you were able to call in. I thought it best we had a short discussion about your . . . ah . . . interest in your brother's estate.'

Alan had taken the seat towards which he had been waved by a pudgy hand. Mr Lloyd had smiled his secretive banker's smile.

'When you called previously, you raised the matter of a certain cheque which you had discovered among your brother's effects in your aunt's house. You suggested we had been . . . er . . . remiss in not finding it and calling in the sum in question. It was, I believe, in the sum of . . .'

'Five thousand pounds.'

'Ah yes.' Mr Lloyd placed the tips of his fingers together in a manner he seemed to regard as sagacious. 'Well, we have now duly presented the cheque and it has been returned.'

'I don't understand.'

'*Returned*,' Mr Lloyd repeated, with satisfaction. 'It would seem the . . . ah . . . debt in question has been cancelled.'

'I still don't understand.'

Mr Lloyd's expression suggested that was hardly his fault. Smugly he said, 'It would seem that the company on whom the cheque was drawn — Farrier Enterprises — deny that any liability arises, because your brother, Mr Fearnley, had agreed not to present the cheque.'

'It was still in his possession,' Alan argued.

'But never presented. I telephoned the people in question, and I was led to understand that Mr Fearnley had written to the chairman of Farrier Enterprises — a Mr Edsel — agreeing that he would not cash the cheque. So, I'm afraid the estate will not be . . . ah . . . swollen by that amount after all. What you discovered, in fact, was quite worthless.'

The thought obviously pleased Mr Lloyd; he obtained even more pleasure from telling Alan so. Alan frowned. 'Did this man Edsel explain the circumstances behind the drawing of the cheque?'

'I thought it not my business to ask the question,' Mr Lloyd replied smoothly. 'I am satisfied that there is documentary evidence to show your brother agreed not to obtain payment, and that, in effect, will cancel any liability that arose between the parties. I shall, of course, in my capacity as executor of the will ask for a copy of the letter in question, but if you have any further enquiries to make in the matter, I would suggest you approach Mr Edsel yourself, in person.'

'I think,' Alan said slowly, 'I'd better do just that.'

Mr Lloyd lifted one shoulder and sniffed. In his consideration, the journey would be a waste of time.

And perhaps it was destined to be, but there were other

reasons why Alan had decided to drive to Bristol that afternoon for an interview with Charles Edsel. It was not merely the matter of the cheque, though he was curious about it. He felt he needed to get away from the valley: he felt echoes of an old claustrophobia gathering around him, echoes that were distorted by confusions in his mind generated by Edwards's persistent claim that Jeff had been murdered, by Danny Elias. He felt hemmed in by Edwards's words, unable to weigh them with any rationality, affected by the man's obsessive beliefs, afraid of their possible truth and yet wary of accepting them because of Edwards's own background.

Additionally, there was the pressure he felt in merely being in the valley again. It was as though he was slipping back into an existence he had thought he had discarded, like a worn-out skin. But it was still there, and it was beginning to stifle him again.

The waters of the Severn were grey and heavy under the stormy sky as he crossed the bridge and headed towards Bristol. His appointment with Edsel was for three-thirty: he would be in good time for it.

Farrier Enterprises Ltd were located in offices in the Gloucester Road. Alan managed to find a parking place in a side street only a short walk away from the road: he presented himself at the brand-new office building that had been raised among the huddle of older, seedier premises at precisely three-twenty-five. The company he wanted was based on the third floor; the carpets were expensive, the furniture modern, but the staff were few in number, and Alan wondered what kind of business Charles Edsel carried on.

The man himself was impressive enough.

He was perhaps fifty years of age, well-dressed in a grey suit and delicate pink shirt. His hands had been carefully manicured, his hair carefully groomed, and the even tan of his skin suggested he spent regular hours abroad or under a sun lamp. It was clear that for him initial impressions were important: his handclasp was firm and convivial, and his welcome generous. He waved Alan to a seat and took out a pipe. It seemed to add an air of solidity to him; perhaps he was in the kind of business where the impression of solidity was a necessary one.

'Now, then, Mr Fearnley, what can I do for you?' He puffed heartily on the pipe, screwing his eyes slightly as he watched Alan. 'I explained to the bank manager over the phone about the cheque that your brother was still holding.'

'That's right, but I was somewhat puzzled about it.'

'I have the letter he sent me,' Edsel said. He drew open the drawer in the desk in front of him and took out a slim file. 'Perhaps you'd like to see it.'

Alan nodded, and Edsel passed the file across to him. Inside was a single page letter; the handwriting would be Jeff's but there was no familiarity in it for Alan. He could not now remember when last he had seen Jeff's handwriting, and the thought depressed him. The letter was short, and to the point.

Dear Mr Edsel

I've had time to think things over. I've decided not to go through with the deal. I've still got the cheque somewhere, but I'll destroy it now. Thanks for the offer, anyway.

Yours sincerely,
Jeff Fearnley.

Alan looked up: Charles Edsel was watching him thoughtfully. He removed the pipe from his mouth. 'I'm surprised he retained the cheque at all.'

'It was in a drawer,' Alan replied. 'I think he'd put it there, and then, being so busy that week, he just never got around, presumably after making up his mind as he says, to doing anything about it.' Alan hesitated. 'Just exactly what *was* the offer you'd made to him? I presume the cheque was a payment of some kind?'

'For *future* services,' Edsel said smoothly. 'A kind of down payment, if you like.'

'And the services?'

Edsel's pipe was not drawing properly; he tapped it against the heel of his hand. 'You've not heard of Farrier Enterprises before, Mr Fearnley?'

'I can't say that I have.'

'We have a number of interests . . . mainly agencies, as a matter of fact, acting in the marketing and distribution industries. But there is an important offshoot which I'm personally trying to build up. It's image marketing.'

'I'm not sure I know what that means.'

Charles Edsel smiled. 'Let me put it like this. In the entertainment business—and the word *entertainment* covers a wide range of activity—it's essential that those people in the front line maintain an image. The burnishing of that image, the protection and development of that image, that's the kind of line I've been trying to develop. I've been pretty successful too. A couple of recording stars, a few actors—but you have to be on the look-out all the time for something new, where you can really strike into something fresh and developing, and . . . likely to make a lot of money. Sport is the obvious answer—if you hit the right sport.'

Alan began to understand. 'You saw in the game of darts—'

'Something new, something interesting, and something completely undeveloped.' Edsel made a deprecating gesture with his hand. 'The fact is, they're amateurs, all of them, in the darts world. They don't know, they don't *appreciate*, the kind of gold-mine they're sitting on. All right, it's been in the twilight world of the local pub for decades, but suddenly there's a new excitement in the air. Television has come on the scene, discovered the game, and it's hitting mass markets. Its not just the *aficionados* who are interested: little old ladies, youngsters, the middle classes, they're all getting hooked on the game. And the sponsors know it—so the cash is beginning to flood in. Within five years it will be a moneyspinner. And that's where I wanted to come in.'

'As an image builder?'

'Provided there was someone around whose image I could mould.' Edsel nodded thoughtfully. 'That was your brother. You see, he had things going for him. It was quite clear he was as near invincible at the game as anyone around could be at the moment. And he was a reserved young man, a good-looking lad who televised well. His commitment at the board was total, and he could be a bit of a bastard too—but he usually managed to get the howls on his side. He had something I could have built on: he had a . . . *presence*. It was the kind of presence that could beat an opponent, even when Jeff wasn't playing well.'

Alan thought of Freddy Thomas's narrow face and cold, committed eyes. His commitment had never been able to overcome Jeff's presence; Alan knew what Edsel was talking about. 'So you approached Jeff?'

Edsel nodded. 'That's right. I rang him, arranged to meet him, we had a talk. Then he came up here to Bristol, for a longer, more detailed chat. What it boiled down to was this: I offered him my expertise in setting him up, properly, as an *entertainer*. It meant he would have to trust me, allow me to dictate to him where he should go, how he should act, dress and live. His programme would be controlled by me—with some other professional advice, of course, and in return I'd bring him contracts that would double his income within the year, bring him away from a pokey living in that valley of his and set him up for life. I told him I'd make him *money*, Mr Fearnley.'

'How did he react?'

Edsel drew thoughtfully on his pipe. 'He was a rather cautious boy. He was . . . reluctant. He wanted time to think things over, but we talked a little more, and I produced a few examples for him in the entertainment world, and he was, I thought, convinced. We started talking in terms of a contract—and I thought a down payment would make his wavering cease.' His eyes flickered towards Alan suddenly. 'I *wanted* that brother of yours, Mr Fearnley. He could have made us both a great deal of money.'

'The down payment was the cheque?'

'That's right. And he took it, said that when I'd got the contract made out he'd sign for me. And then he went back to Wales. He had a series of appearances due that week. Then . . . well, it was all a bit unpleasant really. I picked up the newspaper, about five days later, and read about the accident. I'd tried to contact him the previous day, to tell him the contract was ready and we ought to get together, but he was away for a match. And then there it was: a car crash. I was a bit shaken, you'll understand. Then, when I went in to the office, there was a letter waiting for me. This letter. It was rather a shock.'

'He'd written it the day he died?'

'Then or thereabouts.'

Alan picked up the envelope. The postmark was smudged and unreadable, but it could have been a Swansea postmark. He put it back in the file. 'You don't know why Jeff changed his mind?'

Edsel shook his head. 'I don't know that he was ever really committed to the proposal. I *thought* he was when I last saw him, but I seemed to detect a certain uneasiness all the while. Maybe he didn't trust me.' Edsel smiled deprecatingly. 'Maybe I sold the whole thing too hard. He was just a valley boy, working in a sport that traditionally had been locally based. I suspect the whole thing was just a bit too . . . big for him?' He sighed dramatically, and picked up the file, put it back in the drawer with an air of finality. 'Sad, though. I could have given him a whole new style of living, and he could really have *been* someone. The sky, as they say, would have been the limit. Instead . . .'

Instead, it had ended in the darkness on a mountain road.

II

The atmosphere was still heavy when Alan left the offices of Farrier Enterprises. A storm was possible: a violent downpour would be welcome, to wash away the sultriness of the skies. It would also relieve the dull headache Alan was suffering from. He was not certain its origin was physical—tensions were growing inside him, uncontrollably, and they kept him from an immediate return to the valley now. Instead, he made his way to the offices of Emburey Associates.

The pert-nosed secretary seemed surprised to see him, but that was understandable: he had been away for several days, and had left no word as to when he was returning. She seemed flustered by his appearance, rushing into his office ahead of him as though to check his desk had been dusted. When she asked if he had any instructions for her, he merely asked for a cup of tea.

He put his head back on the chair and closed his eyes. The ache in his skull was a dull throbbing that extended past his temples and around to the back of his head. His scalp prickled and moved and there was the sound of distant thunder beyond Avonmouth. The city needed rain.

He needed more than rain. He needed an order in his life, a settlement of questions, an understanding and a decision about now, and the future. But somehow it was all entwined and encircled by the past: at a time when he needed to concentrate on what he should do about Emburey Associates and Diana and the whole Sunski mess, in order to regularize his own future, his mind was seething with the suspicions that Nick Edwards had implanted in his brain, and with the old, strangling demands of a house in the valley he had left. The thunder growled again, nearer now, and he opened his eyes. The secretary was standing in the door, holding a cup of tea in her hand. She seemed scared.

'What's the matter?' Alan asked.

She ran a nervous pink tongue over her generous mouth. 'Its Mr Emburey . . . he's been on the phone. He . . . he asked if you were in and I told him . . . I didn't know whether you wanted to see him, but—'

'Is he on the way?'

She came forward, putting the teacup on his desk in front of him. 'He's been seeing a client at Temple Meads, and he's making his way back to the office now. He . . . he told me to tell you he insists you wait for him. He . . . he shouldn't be very long.'

Peter Emburey's insistence must have been striking, to scare the girl this way. Alan suspected she feared dire consequences for herself if she allowed him to leave before Emburey arrived. He leaned forward, picked up the cup. 'All right, that's fine. I'll wait for Mr Emburey. Er . . . have you got any codeine?'

Ten minutes later he had opened the file that he had last looked at when the solicitor Stevenson had visited him. It seemed a long time ago, but it was only a matter of days. Even so, to allow the days to slip past in this way was an admission of weakness on his part. The problems would not go away, merely by being ignored: Stevenson was still pursuing his investigations into Sunski and Fernline International, and the accounts still remained with Alan Fearnley, awaiting his audit. And Peter

Emburey was still breathing fire, angry at the delay, unwilling to concede that for Alan a problem even existed.

He arrived twenty minutes later: doors banged in the outer office, and he swept in imperiously, throwing a briefcase across the room on to a vacant chair and dragging off his jacket to throw that, unceremoniously, after the briefcase.

'This bloody weather! If there's anything I can't stand it's this kind of humidity. I need a drink. May I?'

The question was a formality, for he was already opening the cabinet, taking out the bottle of whisky and pouring himself a generous measure in a tumbler. As he squirted some soda-water into the glass Alan sat quietly behind the desk, watching him. Emburey was about Alan's own age, maybe a few years older, but bigger, more heavily fleshed. He had an air of professional confidence that was useful in financial dealings; his broad, handsome face could light up when he smiled, though there were occasions when the smile could be hard-edged, used to remove the public bite from a remark the recipient knew was deadly. He dressed well, lived well, and his business had been successful; he was well known in the City and there had been a time when he had been regarded as one of the country's bright young men, financially. Then things seemed to have petered out; his career had levelled off, he had lowered his sights and tempered his ambitions, and a new harshness had crept into his manner, a demanding pressure that underlay a certain insecurity in his belief in himself. He swung around now, to face Alan. He raised his glass.

'Glad to see you back. Everything sorted out back in the valley?'

'More or less.'

Peter Emburey shook his head. 'You've had me worried. When I phoned, I thought you were playing silly buggers. Still, never mind, now you're back things can get moving. You heard any more from Stevenson?'

Alan shook his head. Emburey grunted in satisfaction, and sipped at his whisky. 'Good. You saw him, of course . . . he'll still be ferreting around, but we can head him off once you get those audited accounts out. Can you give me a date?'

Alan hesitated. 'I'm not sure I can.'

Emburey stared at him. 'What the hell is that supposed to mean?'

'I'm not sure I can give you a date, because . . . well, there are certain questions raised by the accounts which will—'

'Now look here!' Emburey leaned forward over the desk, gesturing with his glass, and a quantity of whisky slopped out, splashing on the file Alan had in front of him. 'Let's get things clear. Sunski *needs* to have those audits prepared soon. It's necessary to have them to raise other finance, and it's too damn late to go pussyfooting elsewhere! Hell's flames, Alan, you've had them a month! Any questions you've had to ask must have been answered by now.'

'That's the problem,' Alan said quietly. 'The questions—most of them—have been answered. But they raise other, ethical issues. And that's why—'

'Ethics.' Peter Emburey's eyes were watchful as he stared at Alan. His features seemed to have darkened, and his mouth was hard. 'It's a word which has always seemed to me to be a refuge for a weak man who is unwilling to take a risk.'

'All business involves risk, Peter, and I suspect that some of the risks taken by Sunski have been unwise.'

'Unwise.' Emburey's mouth twisted unpleasantly. 'I think you'd better start to spell out just what you see as the problem, my friend.'

Alan glanced at the papers in front of him. 'It stems from Stevenson's visit, I suppose—although I'd seen the problem before then. I'd already asked the questions he's now asking.'

'I told you—spell it out!'

Alan took a deep breath. 'All right, I'll do just that. When Mr Stevenson called, he gave me a little lecture.'

'He's inclined that way,' Emburey sneered.

'He lectured me on my duty as an auditor. He stressed that since other people would be relying upon statements I made in the audited accounts, I had a public duty to make no misleading statements. That duty includes the necessity to obtain answers when my . . . suspicions are aroused.'

'Suspicions.' Emburey rolled the word around his tongue, testing it. He inspected the amber liquid in his glass. His voice was quiet. 'Suspicions about what, Alan?'

'About the whole background to Sunski Ltd, and the attempts made to overcome problems arising out of its disastrous takeover of Villa Franchises Ltd.'

'I think you're overstating things somewhat—I wouldn't have described the Villa Franchises set up as a disastrous venture.'

'I would,' Alan said crisply. 'You lost the confidence of IATA, and ended up with bad publicity in a Sunday newspaper and an indebtedness of £250,000.'

Peter Emburey stared at him, a thin smile on his lips. He appeared to be slightly amused at what Alan had said, but there was no smile in his eyes: rather, they held a hint of calculation at odds with the easy confidence he still attempted to project. 'I think you've got things a bit mixed up, Alan. Or was it a slip of the tongue? *I* lost the confidence of IATA?'

'Ella Shore did,' Alan replied. 'And isn't that the same thing?'

Peter Emburey finished his whisky, rose, and poured himself another drink. He loosened his shirt collar, dragged his tie down. 'I'm not clear what you're getting at. Ella and I were married when Sunski was started, but it was always her business. Then, when we were divorced, that was that. I have no involvement with Sunski. Indeed, it would have been, as you put it, *unethical* for me to do so, since my company was auditing the accounts. Somewhat incestuous, if not exactly illegal.'

'I'm not at all certain you're being entirely frank with me.'

'Oh, for God's sake, Alan, what the hell are you trying to say?' Emburey's flash of temper might have been real. 'If I give you assurances—'

'They might not be good enough. Look here, Peter, the fact of the matter is I *had* to do some digging into Sunski as soon as I knew Stevenson and his hotelier clients were howling for payments, and there was some doubt about whether the line of credit negotiated for Sunski would stand up! And as soon as I did start digging some curious facts emerged!'

'All right, let's have them.'

'Your ex-wife, Ella Shore, stayed in Sunski and worked at it; you pulled out after the divorce. But looking at the directorate of Sunski doesn't get anyone very far, because it's only the subsidiary of a holding company, registered not in England but in America. That's the first question I asked myself: when was that holding company formed, and who are the directors?'

'Alan—'

'No, let me finish. Sunski got into trouble with IATA and that could have spelled death for it. But it was lucky—it managed to get a line of credit to the extent of £200,000 from Continentalbank. And it began to draw on the security of that lifeline in 1979.'

'So where's the problem?' Emburey interrupted fiercely.

'The problem is this. I've been making enquiries into the activities of Continentalbank. They are surprisingly, shall we say, limited? In fact, the only office they hold in this country is a small one in Market Harborough, and it never seems to be open. Moreover, the only dealings it's undertaken would seem to have been an attempt, two years ago, to sell Eurobank certificates in units of £10,000 — which was held to be an illegal operation. No action followed — it was just a try-on. The fact is, legally, it was never a *bank* as such, and it was shown it had never claimed to be.'

'So there was nothing illegal in it.'

'So far,' Alan said grimly. 'But let's get back to Sunski. They kept their heads above water with a line of credit from an organization that *sounded* like a bank, even though it wasn't one. Who negotiated that line of credit?'

'I don't see that it is of any importance,' Emburey said snappishly.

'I think it is. I made enquiries, as any auditor should if he has doubts about the financial viability of an organisation like Continentalbank. And once I'd cleared away the miasma of interlocking directorates, sleeping partners, the whole mish-mash of worthless prospectuses and corporate identities, I came up with the core of the whole affair. A company called Fernline International. It's the company that negotiated the line of credit with the bogus bank. But it holds a controlling interest in that bank. And it's also the holding company that was set up to run Sunski!'

'Alan —'

'In other words, when Sunski got into trouble, it turned to Fernline; the parent company got Sunski off the hook by obtaining finance from another of its subsidiaries; that subsidiary, Continentalbank, doesn't have the facilities or the finance to support the line of credit offered to Sunski, and the pigeons are now coming home to roost as the Spanish and Swiss hoteliers gather.'

'Like bloody *vultures*,' Emburey gritted.

'Who are owed a hell of a lot of money,' Alan insisted. 'I knew the kinds of question their legal representative would be asking, so I had to make my own investigation before I produced an audited statement. And if *I* could find out what I did, so could Stevenson.'

'In time, in time, but —'

'And Stevenson would also find out the connection between Sunski and Fernline, Fernline and Continentalbank. The connection was always Ella Shore. *And you*. The fact is, Peter, you've always been deeply involved with her business interests; you have a major holding in Fernline; I've no doubt you helped set up Continentalbank — and by using this business, Emburey Associates, and me, to present audited accounts, the whole thing smacks of fraud!'

Peter Emburey rose angrily to his feet, towering over Alan, his fists clenched on the desk, his darkening features thrust forward menacingly. 'Now just hold on a minute! Let's get things straight. Fraud is a nasty word at the best of times: in the mouth of an accountant, it's nastier. I know the law, and I know the accounting world. Nothing fraudulent has been done.'

'That's a moot point! There have been no illegal transactions yet, but the whole operation is based upon a credit situation that doesn't exist.'

'Credit?' Peter Emburey's lips writhed mirthlessly. 'What the hell are you talking about? What's credit? I tell you, it's merely the confidence that one businessman has in another. It's based on the *belief* there's finance to support a venture — it doesn't matter a damn whether there *is* money there or not — it's just the belief there is. Don't the banks themselves play the same game? What would happen if everyone pulled his money out of the banks? Do you think they could pay up? The hell they could! The fact is, everyone works to the same principle, and I've done nothing essentially different from anyone else. Sunski is

a viable proposition. It's going through a bad patch —
yes, all right, it made a mistake in the Villa Enterprises
venture, but in time even that will pay off handsome
dividends. And that's the important commodity Sunski
needs — time.'

'But I don't —'

'No, you listen,' Emburey said viciously. 'Let me put
you straight. The real estate, the assets held by Sunski are
more than enough to pay off these bloody hoteliers, but
what's the point of that? Should the business be killed off,
liquidated just to satisfy these hungry crows? Sunski needs
time; within three years it could be booming. Your audit
will buy that time. The figures you've got, including the
Continentalbank line of credit, will satisfy the finance
market once they're published over your signature. The
audited accounts can then be used to raise other credit,
we can pay off the hoteliers by drawing on the extended
loans and we're in the clear for a year. A similar operation
next year and we're home and dry and on the verge of a
breakthrough. And there's nothing illegal in it! It's all
about confidence, that's all! And all you've got to do is
prepare those audited accounts!'

Alan Fearnley shook his head. Emburey's voice had
risen in passion; sweat darkened his shirt and there was a
line of droplets on his upper lip. Alan had seen him as a
powerful, confident figure, but he was appearing in a different light now. 'That kind of argument won't wash,
Peter. You use the word *confidence*, but that's precisely
the problem. Our audit would be no more than a
fraud — we'd be telling the world Sunski is healthy, financially, when it isn't. And we'd be saying that at a time
when a senior member of the auditing firm holds a personal interest in Sunski itself. If that isn't as near to fraud
as anything I can think of —'

'Now wait a minute!' Something was happening to
Peter Emburey's face as calculations went on inside his

head, seeking reasons and motivations. 'There's some-thing behind this stance of yours, isn't there? You spout at me about business ethics, but there's something quite dif-ferent bugging you! This isn't about the confidence of the business community at all. This is your way, you sanc-timonious bastard, of getting back at me personally!'

'You haven't listened —'

'I've listened to every word, but it's a load of claptrap! I'd thought you'd faced the truths on your home ground, but I was wrong. Business ethics,' Emburey sneered, his heavy face twisting unpleasantly, his eyes glaring. 'It's got nothing to do with ethics — it's about that bitch of a wife of yours! It's about Diana — that's what's churning your gut!'

Alan stood up, warningly, but Peter Emburey was launched and there was no way of stopping his tirade as he marched around the room angrily, voice raised in bit-terness, passion and frustration curiously intermingled as he saw his business interests endangered by what he con-ceived to be petty revenge. 'Oh, that's what it boils down to — the fact you couldn't keep your bloody wife on the path of marital virtue! Well, let me give you a few facts about that bitch, Diana. In the first place, it was she who made the running, not me! Oh, don't get me wrong — I never really thought it was my good looks that made her hop into bed with me; I always knew exactly what she was after, and if she thought she was conning me at any time, she was greatly mistaken. What she wanted was your ad-vancement, and she had a silly little mind. She thought you needed support; she thought your career needed a boost; and she thought that she was the only one who could do what was necessary. And that meant making up to any man who could help you in your career. Because don't think I was the only one —'

'Emburey, I —'

'Not by a bloody long chalk was I the only one!'

Emburey continued, snorting. 'She sold you down the river a long time ago, my friend — and you know, it was for nothing. *Nothing*. She didn't need to sleep with men to help you get on. You could have, and would have, done it on your own account with no help from her sexual activity. She was too stupid to see that — but no man was going to tell her otherwise. So she slept around and you got on, and now you can't take it! I know you and she have all but split up, so why the hell try to take out your frustrations on me, now? You pursue this petty line, my friend, and you're digging your own professional grave!'

Alan fought to keep his voice under control. 'This has nothing to do with Diana. I meant what I said. I can't lend my name to the kind of fraud you're proposing to undertake.'

'And I don't believe you,' Emburey shouted. 'You're needled because you caught out your little whore of a wife, and you're needled because it's a truth you can't accept.'

'You're wrong!'

'If I *am* wrong, you're even smaller and more stupid than I realized! I think it's time you got something perfectly clear, Fearnley! Sunski must have those accounts audited, and damn quickly. If you won't do them, you're finished with Emburey Associates. Maybe that's what you want, but believe me, it would be suicidal for you. I'd make damn sure you never stepped inside a professional office again. I'd discredit you throughout the accounting world. Because don't think you'd be seen as some kind of knight on a white charger, upholding the ethics of the profession. You'd be seen as a fool rocking the financial boat — and if you believe I couldn't get someone to doctor those figures to make Sunski appear even more respectable, you're crazy.' Emburey paused, then stepped back to the desk, thrusting his empurpled face towards Alan. 'You know what I'm saying, do you? You've got a job to do. Let me down now, and I'll make it known far and wide precisely what smear you're trying to make on me and Sunski—and exactly why you're doing it. There won't be a businessman in the country who won't be sniggering at the story of that silly little blonde wife of yours, bouncing from bed to bed in a vain attempt to buy favours you never needed.'

Alan was silent. He stood glaring at Peter Emburey, fists clenched at his sides, wanting to hit the senior partner in Emburey Associates, but fighting for control. After a few moments Emburey seemed to regain balance himself; some of the colour drained from his features and his body relaxed, tension disappearing as control returned. He turned, walked across to the chair where he had thrown his jacket and took out a cigarette case. He lit a cigarette; there was still a slight tremor in his hand. 'All right,' he said after a few minutes, in a quieter tone, 'I think we've both lost our heads a bit . . . gone too far in what we've been saying. I'm prepared to forget it all—no great harm done. Just some plain talking. And you . . . well, you've got something off your chest too.' He tried to inject some sincerity into his voice, not entirely with success. 'Let's just put it like this Alan. You're wrong in your suppositions. Nothing illegal has taken place. You'll not be countenancing a fraud. You *know* it's a business practice of some antiquity—shipping millionaires have built their fortunes on similar systems: getting a contract to ship freight on a non-existent ship, they got the money to build by flourishing the contract in front of a banker! There's nothing *wrong*. So get those accounts *audited*.' He drew on his cigarette thoughtfully, eyeing Alan. His voice was even softer now, and more menacing because of it. 'But believe me in this, Alan—if you let your personal prejudices, and your domestic problems interfere with this; if you try to suggest that you can't do the work I've asked you to do, all right. But I'll do what I said: I'll spread your story everywhere and make you a laughing-stock, and I'll make sure you'll never get a job in private practice again!'

III

After Peter Emburey had gone Alan sat down, shaking. His mind was a welter of confusion, and he felt as though the conflicts that lay there deprived him of the capacity for rational thought. The suspicions he had harboured about the Sunski operation had been confirmed — Emburey had barely bothered to deny the extent of his involve-ment — but the conviction of the defence put forward by Emburey had surprised him. Peter Emburey really seemed to *believe* that there was nothing wrong in defrauding — as Alan saw it — the merchant banks who would be called upon, on the strength of the audited accounts, to help Sunski out of its financial difficulties. So was Alan's view of the whole situation a reasonable one? Or was it as Peter Emburey himself saw it — the almost subconscious, frus-trated need to strike out at the man who had slept with his wife? When he had first learned of it, Alan had ration-alized the situation in his own mind, knowing it had been Diana who would have pursued the matter, for reasons she saw as reasonable and acceptable. But had he always nursed the desire to hurt Emburey?

His mind swam at the concept of a series of standards and beliefs that were so far out of line with other people's as to render his conduct unacceptable. Had Diana been right, in the way she had behaved? Was Peter Emburey right?

Moving like an automaton, Alan Fearnley left the office and went out to his car, to make the drive back to the Severn Bridge. And when he had crossed into Wales

the storm came at last with a jagged flash of lightning.
The rain teemed down as he drove doggedly along, and
headlights loomed up at him through the darkened
streets like glaring, distressed eyes. After half an hour he
became aware the rain had stopped, and the air was
lighter, cleaner, with a fresh feel to it as he opened the
window, but his own mind was still weighed down with
the doubts that Peter Emburey had placed there.

When he walked into Aunt Matty's she said nothing;
she looked at him with her birdlike eyes pecking for the
truth, and then she turned away, made a cup of tea, set it
down in front of him.

'There's bothered you are.'

'No.' He passed a weary hand over his eyes. 'I'm just a
bit tired, driving to Bristol and back, that's all.'

'What was it you had to go there for? You finished
clearing things over Jeff's estate.'

Alan shook his head. 'No, it was about that cheque that
I went to see a man in Bristol. He'd given Jeff that money
to act as his agent, sort of. But then Jeff wrote to say he'd
changed his mind.' He hesitated, a shadow fluttering
across his mind. He looked up at Aunt Matty. 'Did *you*
know about what Jeff was proposing to do?'

Her eyes held his for several seconds, but he could read
nothing in her glance. 'Don't know what you mean.'

'Jeff had been contacted by Charles Edsel, who wanted
to market him, so to speak. It would have meant a lot of
money for Jeff . . . and you. Did he talk to you about it?'

She shook her head decisively. 'He never said a word to
me about anything of that kind.'

Dispiritedly Alan said, 'It makes no difference,
anyway. Whether he intended at one time to take up
the offer — which would necessarily mean his leaving the
valley — he changed his mind, wrote to Edsel and agreed
not to cash the cheque.'

'He would never have left me,' Aunt Matty said complacently. 'That'll be why he changed his mind, I expect. He could never have gone away, like you did. But even you're back now, aren't you?'

He stared at her. There was another question he had wanted to ask but now, under the pressure of her last comment, it fluttered away, and he lost the thread of what was bothering him. Something was not quite right, something to do with Edsel, but he could not put his finger on it now. He shook his head, and sipped his tea without answering the question she had asked, almost rhetorically.

She sat watching him for a little while, quietly, and he knew her eyes would be probing, seeking out the lines of strain, dwelling upon the reasons for his tiredness and despondency, waiting for the right moment when his defences would be so weak that she would be able to get behind them, get answers to the questions she wanted to ask, and perhaps bind him closer to her by his confidences. It had always been her way; it was so still. She had held Jeff, and now she wanted to recover the one nephew still alive.

'There was a phone call when you were out.'

'For me?'

'Wouldn't leave his name.'

'No message?'

'No. But he had a funny voice. It was all muffled, like, as though he was speaking through bandages or something, or like he had his mouth full. Said he'd ring back. I told him you'd be home tonight.'

Her eyes were curious and questioning; they made him shrug his shoulders and say, 'I can't imagine who it would be.'

But the phone rang at eight that evening and though as Aunt Matty had said the voice was muffled, he recognized it immediately. It was Nick Edwards. He was speaking from a hospital in Pontypridd.

★

The ward sister had a mouth like bent iron and a personality to match. She seemed to imply that any visitor
was to be regarded as something that had just crawled
out, unbidden, from a test tube and might produce
dangerous infection in the pure air of her domain. It was
with considerable reluctance that she allowed Alan entry,
and as she preceded him along the sterile corridor her
back was stiff with starched resentment.

'I can't allow you to stay long. The doctor said you
should be allowed to visit him, though I don't approve of
it because he should be getting rest in his condition, but
you must promise me you won't disturb him, or stay too
long.'

Alan promised, and the ward sister swept on, opening
the door and standing aside to allow him entry. It was a
small, green-painted room, with two single beds. Only
one of them was occupied. The occupant was Nick
Edwards.

He was lying propped up on his pillows. His head was
bandaged, the covering being drawn down beneath his
chin so that only a restricted area of his face — eyes, nose,
mouth — was visible. He had a plaster cast on his right
hand, which seemed to extend up to his elbow, but when
he saw Alan enter the room his eyes were bright, almost
feverish.

'Not too long, now,' the sister warned again, and Alan
nodded and walked forward to stand beside the bed. The
telephone with which Edwards had called him was beside
the bed, plugged into a wall socket. Edwards's eyes strayed to
it, and his mouth moved. 'I phoned a couple of times.'

The restriction of the bandaging muffled his voice.
Alan gestured to his hand and the swathes of bandage.
'What . . . what's the trouble?'

There was a strange triumph in Nick Edwards's eyes. 'A
broken wrist. A few sprung ribs, they tell me — trouble

breathing, you know. And a fractured jaw.'

Alan sat down. 'How did it happen?'

'Been down to Bute Street. Saw a feller. Was walking back to my car and they came on me. Two of them. Big fellers. They didn't say a word; just piled in. There's some cuts and bruises under the bandages, but nothing really serious. They knew what they were about.'

'How do you mean?'

'A frightener. No *serious* injuries. But painful as hell, and a warning that things could be worse. The jaw and the ribs — they were the main things. The wrist, that happened when I fell awkwardly. But they made their point.'

Alan looked at Edwards carefully. 'What was their point?'

'Can't you guess?' Edwards replied, and gave a small sigh, almost as though he had achieved a strange kind of satisfaction.

'Do you know who they were?'

'Never saw them before. Won't again, shouldn't think.'

'So how do you —'

'How do I *know* Danny Elias was behind it?' Edwards's feverish glance was fierce. 'Because it's obvious! I was in Cardiff to see a man who was working for Elias the night your brother died. And I'd only just left him when these two thugs took me. It all fits, Mr Fearnley, it all fits. And in a way it puts the lid on the whole thing.'

'In what way? What did this man tell you?'

Edwards eased himself up on his pillows and grimaced. 'I'd been sniffing around in Swansea and got nowhere; couldn't make any contacts I could use. But then I learned that one of the bouncers who worked for Elias in the Swansea club the night Jeff Fearnley got killed had left Elias, taken a job in Cardiff Docks. So I thought I'd have a word with him. It was instructive.'

'What did he have to say?' Alan asked.

In spite of his pain, Nick Edwards was enjoying

himself. 'This chap — the bouncer — his job was to stay out front, make sure no drunks came in, chat up the local coppers when they make their Saturday night rounds with the dogs and so on. He's the front line, defence and attack if you like. But he didn't spend *all* his time in the front of house. In between the darts match there was a bit of cabaret, and he fancied one of the girls in the group that night. So he went back a few times, to chat her up a bit.'

'So?'

'So he gathered it wasn't all sweetness and light that particular evening.'

'How do you mean?'

Edwards grimaced again, and his left hand strayed up to his bandaged jaw, touching it gingerly. 'The darts players weren't using the proper dressing-rooms — most of them were in makeshift accommodation behind the stage. But Jeff had been given a small room to change in, and relax. The bouncer, he'd gone backstage to see this girl and he walked past Jeff's room. It seems there was a bit of a barney going on in there.'

'A quarrel?'

'A hell of a quarrel.' Edwards could not keep the satisfaction out of his tone. 'Your brother was shouting his head off, but the other one was yelling too, and the language wasn't too choice.'

'What was the quarrel about?' Alan asked.

Edwards shook his head slowly. 'You got to remember — this character had other things on his mind. He just remembers voices raised in anger — what it was all about, he had no idea.'

'What time was this?'

'Again, he couldn't be certain. But early on, he thought. It seems maybe Jeff had been up at the board once, and not thrown too well, and was due again, for his final with Freddy Thomas. And then there was this row — before he went out and beat Thomas, maybe an hour or so later.'

Alan felt vaguely disappointed. 'And is this all you got from the man?'

Anger stained Edwards's eyes. '*All*? But don't you see how important it is? It fits into the pattern—and when you add to it what happened to me tonight—'

Alan shook his head. 'I'm not so sure—'

'Then let me lay it out for you, the way it was,' Edwards said fiercely. 'Your brother went up to Swansea that night in a presentation laid on by Danny Elias. He would be expecting Elias to support him, as usual. But he was off form, not playing well. Now after he arrived, one of two things happened. Either Elias realized Jeff was off form and decided to bet elsewhere, on Thomas probably, or the whole thing was fixed from the start. And my guess is, it was the second.'

'And the quarrel?'

'Jeff worked the first legs, won through so that the odds on Thomas lengthened, and Elias got his bets down. Then Jeff went to his dressing-room. He'd been drinking—that's something the bouncer could confirm too, because it was noticed by quite a few that night that Jeff sank more than usual for such an occasion—and after he'd been drinking he started to brood. Then, when Danny Elias went into the room, maybe to tell him he'd got the bets down and things were going fine, Jeff blew his top. He told Elias he wasn't going through with it.'

'You're suggesting his pride wouldn't let him be beaten by Thomas?'

Edwards nodded. 'He must have told Elias there was no way he was going to play second best to his stablemate. And friend Danny didn't like it. They had a shouting match—Elias told him he stood to lose a lot of money, maybe that this fix would only improve things for Jeff later, in that it would raise interest in what had been developing into a series of one-horse contests—and tempers were really roused.'

'And then?'

Edwards paused. His bright eyes searched Alan's features as though seeking the answers there. He took a deep breath. 'I think your brother finally agreed. He gave in to Elias's bullying.'

Alan stared at the man in the bed. It would, perhaps, have been in character. Jeff Fearnley had spent all his years subjected to the domination of another person; Aunt Matty's bullying would have been less noisy, more subtle than Danny Elias's, but the recipient in each case had been conditioned to doing what he was told. He was susceptible to pressure, in a way that Alan Fearnley himself still was, in spite of his having left the valley fifteen years ago, to escape the smothering inhibitions of a personality and a way of life that denied him freedom of expression and thought. Yes, he could believe that Jeff would have given way to Danny Elias's arguments.

'He went back out to the final, against Freddy Thomas,' Edwards continued, his voice dropping almost to a whisper. 'Elias would have been in the hall, watching. And at first, it would have been all right — Jeff's performance was poor. But then things changed; Thomas was getting a run of bad luck, and Jeff was coming through. Somewhere along that point, somewhere during that game, Jeff changed his mind. Maybe he'd only been toying with Thomas; maybe his bad play had been deliberate; who knows? But I *am* convinced that Jeff was supposed to throw that game, and didn't. And as a consequence, Danny Elias lost a great deal of money.'

Alan regarded the ex-newspaperman steadily for a little while. There had been the ring of conviction in the man's tones, and yet Alan could recall the obsessive nature of his insistence, the first night he had approached Alan in the rain. It was dangerous to take a man's word, when a question of balanced judgement remained. He shook his head, doubtfully. 'It may be as you say it was . . . but where's the proof? Some circumstantial evidence on the mountain, which can be explained away in other terms; a quarrel between Jeff and someone you *think* was Danny Elias . . . It's not enough, you know. It's just not enough.'

Edwards struggled to a more upright position. 'Then what about me, in here, then? Is that something that's just a figment of my imagination? All right, you think I'm over the edge on Danny Elias, that I'm just out to get him because of the past! Maybe that's so—but I *know* he put Jeff away that night. And this proves it! Look, I've not been near Elias—I've watched, but I've stayed in the background. I approached you, but that's all. But no one can make too many enquiries without word leaking back—and Elias will have heard that someone's been asking questions. And when I came down to Cardiff to question that bouncer, that was too much for Elias. I had to be warned off—and that's exactly what happened! This was no mugging—they didn't even try to lift my wallet. This was a *warning*. To stop asking questions about what happened to Jeff Fearnley!'

Alan rose, paced around the room uneasily, biting thoughtfully at his lower lip. 'I don't know. The kind of world you're talking about, it's an unfamiliar one to me. I can't believe that this kind of thing can happen—'

'Believe it,' Edwards rasped. 'I *know*. Hell's flames, I'm feeling it right now! You think I got these bruises falling off a swing?'

Alan stared at him. 'There's still nothing we can take to the police.'

Edwards lay back, sighing. 'Maybe not. But I'm laid up now, and there are still questions that can be asked. The kind of questions that can maybe flush Danny Elias right out into the open.'

'How do you mean?'

The flicker of malicious triumph was back in Edwards's

eyes as he stared past Alan, out towards the window and the dark sky beyond. 'Just background really, simple questions of background, about what happened that night. It'll scare hell out of Elias—he was scared enough to do this to me. Because, you see, I think Elias went a step too far that night.'

'In what way?'

'He got *personally* involved.' Edwards's mouth moved, his lips twitching into a painful smile. 'He got out of his prison sentence last time on appeal, because the evidence against him personally was too thin. But he didn't learn. Or maybe he forgot. *This* time, it's different. I think he exposed himself—personally. It wasn't any thug that killed your brother up there on the mountain.'

'Elias himself?' Alan was puzzled. 'How can you be certain of that?'

Edwards grunted confidently. 'Because that bouncer, he told me something else. Jeff Fearnley didn't drive away from the club alone that night. The bouncer had been backstage, clearing out some troublemakers; he walked back to the front of the house and he saw your brother's car in the street. Someone was getting into the passenger seat. They drove off together.'

Alan stood at the foot of the bed, his hands gripping its rail. 'Was it a man, or a woman?'

'He didn't get a good look—but it was probably a man. And my guess is, it was Danny Elias.' The painful smile twitched again, unpleasantly. 'And a few simple questions could find out—hey?'

CHAPTER 5

I

Simple questions. But were they so simple?

How could any questions be simple when they were bound up in human motivations and relationships, the reactions one person raised in another, hidden thoughts, unspoken words, degrees of rationality personal to the individual?

Aunt Matty. What was the driving force that made her need to cling, dominate, rule those closest to her? The man she had married had become a cypher, a weakling incapable of judgement or decision—though perhaps that was why *he* had married *her*, for he had wanted domination. Alan Fearnley himself had felt the weight of her control, the probing, the insistent demands to be feared and loved in the same heartbeat. He had seen his uncle crumble into subservience and had fled such a fate; but there must have been something in Jeff that had prevented him turning his back on the old lady. The spark of defiance had been missing. The ability to decide.

She sat facing him now across the table, almost crumpled in her chair, dark dress, dark-visaged, with the brown stains of age marking her skin. The eyes were still young, bright, glittering and intelligent, their watchfulness those of a cat searching for an enemy, but her body was small and bony, folds of skin over time-wasted flesh. Or perhaps it was not time that had wasted her body; maybe it had been the effort, the searing necessity to bend others to her will, to remain the centre of a narrow universe of her own creation.

'I had a letter from Mr Lloyd,' she said, her voice

whispering like dry leaves over a pavement. 'He thinks he can get probate fairly quickly, and he'll be able to let me have some of the money on account, like.'

'Take his advice on investment,' Alan said. 'Bank managers are cautious, and usually right.'

'Why not your advice?' she asked, her voice rising a little.

'I won't be *here*, Aunt Matty,' he said as gently as he could.

'Why do you have to leave? For that matter,' she added after a short silence, 'where will you go?'

He could feel the old suffocation, the blankets beginning to envelop him. 'Aunt Matty—'

'No. I'm not a fool. I got eyes, boy, and I listen. That phone call you had with that man Emburey—he rang a couple of times after, you know. I can tell—the tone of voice he used. There's trouble of some kind you're in, and you been running away from it. And you ran *here*, didn't you? Jeff was just an excuse; you had other reasons to come home.'

He wanted to say that this was not his home but the words stuck in his throat as the sharp little eyes bored into him.

'And then there's your wife, too. No contact; no attempt to get in touch, you with her, or her with you. You don't have to tell me about that, boy; it was a mistake, wasn't it, and now you found out, again it was back here you had to crawl and lick your wounds, wasn't it?'

A brief surge of anger took him. 'Animals are allowed to lick their wounds in *private*, Aunt Matty.'

'Privacy isn't for families,' she reprimanded him. 'And families is for helping and caring.'

'Do *you* care, Aunt?' he asked. 'Or, to put it another way, what do you care about?'

She was silent for a little while. There were a few

seconds when he thought she was going to cry, but that was not and never would be her way. She began to smooth the tablecloth in the old, familiar, agitation-controlling gesture, a short fluttering of one hand, brushing away non-existent crumbs. 'I cared when you left, Alan. And I care now, again, and if you go . . .'

It was a new pressure in its way, an unstated, softer demand that reminded him of her advancing years. It was an insidious pressure that he would find hardest of all to resist, for it was based on sentiment, instead of control. He wondered if she had ever had to use such words to Jeff. It came back, then, fluttering from the darker corners of his brain, re-emerging, forming words and questions.

'Aunt—you said Jeff never told you about the offer he had received from Charles Edsel?'

The hand was stilled on the tablecloth. 'That's what I said.'

'You mean, when he was talking to Charles Edsel . . . when he made a visit to Bristol to Farrier Enterprises, he never discussed it with you?'

She rose abruptly, reaching for the teapot and the milk jug. 'I told you. He didn't tell me. I'd better start clearing the table.'

She walked out into the kitchen and Alan rose, following her, frowning. 'I'm a bit confused, somehow. When I told you that Jeff had talked to Charles Edsel, you didn't seem surprised.'

'What was there to be surprised about?' she asked snappishly.

'The fact that he was contemplating leaving the valley to work with Farrier Enterprises, for God's sake!' Alan said in exasperation.

'Don't you take His name like that in this house,' she said, rounding on him. 'And I don't know what you're on about. It doesn't matter anyway; whatever he was doing, whoever he was talking to, in the end he would have come

to me, to talk to *me* about it, and he would never have
left, never have gone the way you did.'

'Because you would have persuaded him to stay,
wouldn't you?' Alan said slowly. 'But this time, you didn't
have to persuade him.'

'That's right,' Aunt Matty said triumphantly. Her eyes
were shining brightly. 'He made up his own
mind — whatever you say he had decided earlier. He
decided to stay. I didn't need to talk to him.'

Alan hesitated. 'So when *did* you learn about the Farrier Enterprises offer?' he asked.

She had turned her back to him; her shoulders were
still, but he was aware of the tension in her small body.
'What are you talking about?' she asked.

'You weren't *surprised* when I told you. You already
knew about it.' He thought back to something the managing director of Farrier Enterprises had said in Bristol. 'It
was Charles Edsel, wasn't it?'

Impatiently she began, 'Hah, what's it all matter—'

'When I saw Edsel in Bristol, he told me he'd tried to
get hold of Jeff, to tell him the contract was ready. But
Jeff was away, at a match. Edsel rang here, didn't he? He
spoke to you, and asked you to pass the message to Jeff.
That's when you knew Jeff was thinking about leaving the
valley, to work with Farrier Enterprises. That's why my
information was no surprise.'

She leaned over the draining unit, began to stack
already dried dishes. 'He called, yes, wanted to speak to
Jeff. I told him Jeff was away, and I asked him if I could
take a message. And he told me about his old contract.'
She turned suddenly to face Alan; her lips were thin, her
expression determined. 'But I knew Jeff would never go
through with such a contract. I knew he would never be
able to leave me and the valley, not the way you did.'

But she was not saying it with the old conviction, the
defiance he knew so well. There was something wrong,

something in her manner he could not understand.

The only name he could put to it was one he had never thought he would be able to use, in connection with Aunt Matty.

Defensiveness.

II

The billboards outside the club had proclaimed in three-inch-high lettering that the first prize was £1500 as a result of the sponsorship of a firm of whisky manufacturers; in the main entrance there were colourful displays of bunting and pictures of Scotland and grouse and antlered stags; the usherettes checking tickets wore mini-kilts and white, off-the-shoulder blouses with twee facsimile daggers patterned on each breast, while from inside the main floor of the club the thunderous version of a highland reel battered the senses with its confusion of cultures: to Alan's ears a pop group with its electric guitars playing Scottish reels on a Welsh stage presented an incomprehensible incongruity. But the wailing and ranting was dying away as the call came again, from the white-suited man with the microphone.

'GAME ON, FOLKS, GAME ON!'

The serious business of the night was about to start.

Alan made his way to the cloakroom. He washed his hands, letting the cold water run on his wrists. He felt oddly warm; it was tension, uncertainty, he knew, but the cause was an unreasoning fear. He had come here alone tonight, and he had questions to ask of Danny Elias, but it was not only the thought of Nick Edwards lying in a hospital bed that bothered him. There was something else. It could have been the fear of looking foolish; it was possibly the fact he still only half believed that there was

anything substantial behind Edwards's obsessive alle-
gations. Yet there was something else too: it may be he
had questions to ask, but the answers might not be the
ones he wanted.

He dried his hands and made his way slowly to the
main doors leading into the night club.

It was bigger than the Black Cat, a longer room, but in
some respects very similar in its layout. The dais on the
left still held the instruments used by the pop group, but
the young men themselves had now deserted it. Below the
dais, the main floor itself was packed with small tables
where men and women sat, beer glasses and basket meals
in front of them, with the narrow communicating
channels between them perambulated by more mini-
kilted waitresses. Above them ran a gallery where meals
were being served at tables giving a bird's eye view of the
proceedings, but from there on the resemblance to the
scene at the Black Cat ended. For this was a grander,
more prestigious event. The end of both galleries had
been screened off and batteries of lamps had been placed
there to glare whitely down on the diamond-shaped stage
erected against the far end wall. Under the hot television
lights, the white suit of the compère for the evening shone
and glittered with subdued sequins, and to his left a
simpering blonde in a shimmering evening gown manipu-
lated an electronic scoreboard which gave her as little to
do as possible: mathematically superfluous, she merely
added colour and glamour to the mechanical control
unit.

The darts board was a small oasis, its enhanced colours
bright against a dark background, its steel-coloured
numbers glittering under the lights. To the right of the
board was a video unit which featured the board itself: as
each dart thudded into the board it could be seen on the
video unit by almost everyone in the room. The compère
would be calling the scores, but the *aficionados* in the

audience were able to read them, for themselves, even as the darts embedded themselves in the board.

And above the whole scene, set back in the centre of the hall itself, a vast, slowly circling lighting unit revolved, sending pools of subdued colours moving over the whole of the floor, changing faces to varying subdued colours and shades, a flickering charade, a parade of coloured fantasies against the shadowed backgrounds where the night people of the club management moved.

Alan stood on the thickly carpeted steps, staring down at the scene. Behind him, the long bar was virtually deserted, and the waitresses also were taking a brief respite, for the tension had risen as the two men facing the board flicked their darts, silver flashes under the glaring television lights, into the board. It was a re-run of what Alan had seen and experienced in the Black Cat, and yet more: the presence of the camera units, left and right, the swinging boom, the crews moving along their cleared, pre-organized path directly towards the perspiring combatants, it all sharpened the atmosphere, heightened the tension, and Alan knew with a sudden clarity how it was that Jeff could never have allowed himself to be beaten. Not in this kind of situation; not with all the pressures and the demands of this howling crowd. Nick Edwards had said professional pride would have made him change his mind, whatever he might have agreed to do, and Alan knew, clearly, that the exnewspaperman had been right.

'*And it's a single three, for a double eight,*' the compère chanted. The first dart flashed, the crowd bayed; a second, silver movement in the air was followed by a groan, and then as the third dart thudded home, pandemonium broke loose, the compère's 'DOUBLE EIGHTTT!' almost drowned in the volume of excited, admiring sound. The successful player was facing his audience, yellow sweater shining, wide grin recorded, gap-toothed, by the television cameras boring in, and taped music thundered in the background, underlying the roar of the crowd, adding a pulsating dimension to the excitement that served to further heighten the passion exploding in the room.

Alan recognized it as sheer theatre, but still felt his blood quicken.

He stood on the steps and slowly surveyed the room. The revolving patchwork of lights made it difficult for him to pick out the faces he was seeking, but he knew roughly where they were likely to be. Freddy Thomas was playing tonight, so he would be near the stage, somewhere, in the roped-off area to the right, where competitors and their guests sat. Alan walked down the steps, checking carefully the people at each table, and when he reached the silken ropes he finally made out the table he wanted. There were some unfamiliar faces, men and women, but among them were Marilyn, her husband Jim Carter, Freddy Thomas and Danny Elias. He lifted the rope, to step under it, and a beefy hand descended on his.

'Sorry, sir. Only card holders in there.'

He was big, heavy, with curly hair and cold eyes.

'I want to talk to some people over on that table.'

'Sorry, sir.'

Alan hesitated, then nodded and moved away, back towards the wall and clear of the tables. The big man watched him for a few moments, then turned away. Alan leaned against one of the pillars supporting the gallery and observed the table, and the people he sought.

Marilyn was dressed in pale blue, an off-the-shoulder dress, and her skin gleamed under the hot lights. She seemed relaxed, happier than she had previously been in her husband's company, and Jim Carter himself seemed to be in good humour. He was laughing at something Danny Elias had said, his head thrown back, the grey wings in his thick, curly hair almost indistinguishable. He was wearing the same clothes he had worn at the Black

Cat, but what was it Elias had said about Carter being superstitious? Certainly he would have little cause for anxiety tonight, if the betting was anything to go by: Freddy Thomas was a clear favourite to win the finals.

Now there was no Jeff Fearnley to contend with.

Danny Elias was sprawled in his chair, confident, a glass of champagne in his left hand. Under the lights his lean face seemed younger than Alan remembered, even though those same lights exposed the creamy skin under his thinning hair. He was talking in a desultory manner to Freddy Thomas, who sat beside him. Thomas himself had not changed: the television world affected him in no way. He was the same person Alan had seen in the New Inn, and Alan knew now that there was no essential distinction between what had happened in that local pub that evening, and what Thomas would be wanting to do tonight, to his opponent. At the Black Cat there had been a suspicion that Thomas had played with his opponent, in order to ram home the fact of his superiority at the last; equally, in the New Inn Thomas had deliberately needled his young brash challenger in order to make his humiliation the greater. It would be the same tonight: for there was a streak of committed cruelty in Freddy Thomas. It lay glinting behind his eyes; it would appear in the thin sneer that occasionally touched his mouth. Freddy Thomas needed to win, and at the same time trample the man he played against.

It must have been an agony for the man, these last few years, to suffer defeat after defeat at the hands of Jeff Fearnley.

The next pair were rising to make their way to the diamond of light, and a chanting arose from a section of the crowd. They were supporters of the man in the white sweater, one hand clutching his paunch as he climbed up to face the board. Alan recognized him: 'Goliath' Harry Dickson, the man Thomas had defeated at the Black Cat.

He was first to throw tonight, and he started with three treble twenties. It was the best possible start, in what Alan understood to be a play-off for the third prize of the evening, but during the next twenty minutes he realized that Dickson was not showing the kind of form he had displayed when he had run Freddy Thomas so close. As he lost the first leg, there was the thunder of feet under the tables, and Danny Elias was leaning forward, saying something to Freddy Thomas. The dark, lean Welshman glanced towards his erstwhile opponent and shrugged; grinning, Elias got to his feet and made his way out of the roped-off area. Alan watched him go; he was headed for the cloakroom. Alan waited for a few minutes, and then followed him.

When the door closed behind him the uproar from the main floor was muted, a muffled, indistinct sound that seemed very distant from the quietness of the cloakroom. Danny Elias was the only other person in the cloakroom; he was washing his hands as Alan entered. Alan stood there for a moment, watching Elias, then the bookmaker caught a glimpse of him in the mirror. He turned his head. A slight frown of non-recognition crossed his face, and then he smiled easily. 'Fearnley! Didn't recognize you for a moment. Getting hooked on the game already, is that it?'

Outside, there was a temporary lull in the muted sound. 'Something like that,' Alan replied.

Elias stared at him enquiringly and a slight unease appeared in his eyes. He turned away to dry his hands under a hot-air dryer. Punching the button on the machine, he said, 'If I'd known you were coming in tonight, I could have arranged for you to join us. Are you alone?'

'I'm alone.'

'Then why not—'

'I was up at the hospital in Pontypridd last night.'

The sound of the dryer disturbed the short silence that

fell. Danny Elias was half turned away from Alan. Casually he said, 'You made that statement as though it should mean something to me.'

'I think it should.'

Elias waited until his hands dried, then he turned to the mirror above the washbasin. He adjusted his tie with care, flicked an invisible piece of fluff from his shoulder and turned to look at Alan. 'Something bothering you, Fearnley?'

'I was up at the hospital talking to a man called Nick Edwards.'

'Never heard of him.' Elias made as though to walk past Alan, but when Alan put out a hand to restrain him the bookmaker stopped dead. He stared at Alan's raised hand, and then looked up. His face was stiff, his expression wooden. 'If you got something to say, Fearnley, say it — but don't try to lay a hand on me.'

'Or you'll break my arm, like you fixed Edwards?' Alan jeered.

Elias flickered his tongue over dry lips. 'Just what is that supposed to mean?'

'It means that Nick Edwards is someone you've known for years; that I know about his involvement with you; and that when he started asking too many questions too close to home you had some of your thugs put him in hospital.'

'You're talking a load of rubbish!'

'I don't think so. What I want to know, Elias, is just *why* you felt it necessary to give Edwards that warning.'

'I don't need to say anything to you —'

'I think you do! Edwards was asking some uncomfortable questions about that night at Swansea, about the quarrel you had with my brother, and for that you had him beaten up. That means I have an interest, and that means you *do* need to start talking to me —'

'Listen!' Elias took a step forward, his jaw jutting

angrily, a pulse beginning to beat in his temple as his temper rose. 'You'd better understand something. I don't know what the hell has got into you, but you're making a big mistake listening to wild tales from that nut case Edwards. He's got more than a few screws loose, if you believe me — all right, he put some pressure on me a few years ago, and that was his job, but ever since he's had some crazy ideas about how his wife died and what the hell else, and he's been persecuting me. You know that? *Persecuting* me! And there's just so much of that a man can stand.'

'So you put him in hospital!'

Elias shoved a stubby finger at Alan, prodding the air in a violent gesture. 'If I did, it's my business, and nothing to do with you. But if you want to play the same kind of silly games, I can do the same for you. Now get out of my way!'

He thrust himself violently past Alan; taken momentarily off balance, Alan staggered and lurched sideways. By the time he recovered, Elias was already outside the cloakroom and making his way up the stairs. There were two men at the top of the stairs, hands clasped behind their backs. Alan guessed they were employees of the club; he also guessed that if he pursued Elias now, he would only succeed in getting himself ejected from the club. Scowling, he walked up the stairs slowly. When he reached the top and moved towards the gallery steps, he could see Elias threading his way back towards his group beyond the silken ropes. Alan moved back to his station beside the pillar. He stood there indecisively, frustrated by the feeling he had lost his chance to face things out with Elias, and ask the questions he wanted to. A subdued rumble of approving sound arose as Harry Dickson moved up to begin the last leg of his battle for third place.

The big man twirled his dart nervously as he squinted at the board. '*And it's all to play for!*' incited the compère. Dickson fired his first dart and the throaty rumble came as he scored treble twenty and followed it with another. The third dart hit the wire and bounced out, to a groan of disappointment. It was not going to be Harry Dickson's evening.

Nor would it be Alan's, unless he could have another opportunity to needle Danny Elias, for he knew the man was still aware of his presence. Elias sat in profile to Alan, Freddy Thomas's shoulders in front of him, but he knew that Alan was still watching, and waiting. The crowd roared, and Alan's attention was momentarily diverted back to the diamond stage where Dickson's opponent had just secured a maximum, and then, when he looked back to the table inside the ropes Marilyn was staring at him.

He caught her glance, raised his hand in a half-salute, and she grinned, and waved. Next moment she turned to her husband and said something; Carter looked up sharply, caught sight of Alan and managed a smile. A few words more from Marilyn and he shrugged; she rose quickly and made her way from the table towards Alan.

She stood just inside the silken rope. 'I didn't know you were coming tonight!'

'Last minute decision.'

'Are you alone?' When he nodded, she grinned. 'Well, come and join us. Don't worry about *him*,' she gestured towards the man who had prevented his entry earlier, and who was now watching the conversation with a vague interest. 'I'll fix that.' She went over to him, spoke swiftly, he nodded, and walked away. 'There,' she added on her return. 'He's gone to fetch you a chair. Now come on in.'

She lifted the rope, and he ducked underneath, then followed as she led the way across to the table. He stood there for a few moments until the chair was brought for him, and as the roars grew around him to a crescendo, welcoming the beating that Harry Dickson was getting at the oche, he sat down.

Danny Elias sent one swift glance in his direction and its message was clear. The man sitting in front of him, however, stared at Alan with unveiled hostility. Freddy Thomas's eyes were cold; it may well have been that he was gearing himself up to his final match tonight, but Alan gained the impression that the hostility in that glance was in part, at least, directed towards him.

III

'*So it's Big Jimmy, folks, the wizard from the Outback and all set to go for the big one tonight! Let's give him a hand, and all the encouragement he needs to show us the form we know he can produce!*'

The crowd bayed its approval as the popular Australian stood forward, raising his large hands above his head, darts flashing in his left hand. A big, heavy-breasted man, dewlapped and with a face heavy as a sandbag, he still sported the black Zapata moustache Alan had noted at the last contest, and the silver buttons on his black shirt gleamed and shone under the hot television lights.

'*And facing the man from Australia on this night of nights, we've got the boy from the valleys, so often the bridesmaid and never yet the bride—but is this his night? I give you, our own, ice-cold Freddy Thomas!*'

The noise increased in its intensity and a solid drumming of feet began, a hammering of empty glasses on the tables. The chanting was rhythmic, but it was as though Thomas hardly heard it. He stood at the oche, with his unfashionably cut hair and thin, hollow-cheeked features, in stark contrast to the beefy Australian at his elbow. Neither man looked at the other; both seemed to be concentrating inwardly, and as the noise increased the compère called into his microphone, '*The first prize this evening is a magnificent fifteen hundred through the generosity of our sponsors, and where's it about to go—Australia or Wales? This is where we find out—it's three legs to five-oh-one, five minutes between each leg—and may the best man win.* GAME ON!'

Big Jimmy had won the advantage of throwing first and had stepped forward; as he did so, Thomas said something to him and the big Australian scowled, muttered a reply and then steadied himself for his first three darts.

'Freddy'll have said something to try to needle him,' Marilyn muttered in Alan's ear.

He had certainly not managed to upset the Australian's concentration, nevertheless: the darts flashed to the board for the compère to exult in a maximum one hundred and eighty, and Big Jimmy gave his opponent a glassy stare as he made way at the oche. Freddy Thomas hardly seemed to notice him: he stepped forward, his lean frame stooping slightly forward as he measured distances and angles, and then in three swiftly placed throws he matched Big Jimmy's maximum with one of his own.

'*The best possible answer, folks, and we've got a game on here!*'

Jim Carter turned to Alan and grinned, shaking his head. 'He's right there, it's going to be quite a match, I reckon, but my money's still on Freddy. He's really hyped up tonight—a lot different from the Swansea final.'

Danny Elias heard the comment and his back stiffened; Alan could tell the man wanted to turn his head and look at him but was willing himself not to do so. Alan leaned forward. Amid the din around the floor, his words could be heard only by Elias himself. 'Walking away from me isn't going to solve anything, Elias. I want to know why you put Edwards into hospital. And I want to know why you quarrelled with my brother, that night at Swansea.'

The back of Elias's neck had reddened with anger, but he made no reply. Alan leaned back again, and from the corner of his eye he noticed Marilyn glancing at him. A few moments later, as a roar broke from the audience in approval of another big score from Big Jimmy, she said to Alan, 'You're looking a bit grim about something. Is anything the matter?'

Alan stared at her for several seconds, and then he nodded slowly. 'I think I've got the proof we need.'

Her eyes widened. 'About . . . about Jeff's death?' Her glance slipped past him to Danny Elias. 'I don't understand . . . I can't believe.'

'It all fits together—just a few loose ends.'

She shook her head slightly, as though bemused, and then she glanced sideways, hesitantly, at her husband. Alan put out a hand, but it was too late to stop her. She leaned across to Jim Carter and began to whisper urgently in his ear. Alan looked at Danny Elias; the man's concentration seemed to be directed to the stage but Alan guessed otherwise. Marilyn touched Alan's hand.

'Wait for a few minutes,' she said in a low voice.

Beyond her, Jim Carter was staring at Alan. His skin seemed to have taken on a greyish tinge and his mouth sagged at the corners. But his glance seemed to suggest he considered he was looking at a madman.

A rumbling began from the audience and Alan was aware that Big Jimmy was standing at the oche, poised to throw. The compère moved to one side, his sequinned suit flashing and coruscating in the television lights. '*Well, here we are, the first moment of truth! One hundred and fifty-six, so a three-dart exit is on!*'

The Australian took up his square set stance, his heavy face set, piggy eyes screwed up in concentration, and then he thrust his heavy body into the throw with his characteristic grunt. The dart thudded into the board and the crowd called encouragement as the video unit showed a treble twenty. The heavy body lurched again, but Alan noted that the arm was still locked and controlled, automatic in its steeliness, flicking the second dart into the board. The noise died after an initial roar, and the compère's call of a second treble twenty: in the silence, Freddy Thomas stood still, glaring at the board as his opponent steadied himself for the final dart. It flickered through the air, and the sound of excited approval all but drowned the compère's crow. *'Double eighteen and it's first game to the man from the Outback!'*

Marilyn touched Alan's arm and stood up. Her husband rose with her. As Alan pushed back his chair Danny Elias turned his head to look at him; the cold, bitter hostility in the glance persuaded Alan at that moment that any doubts he might have had about Elias's capacity to commit murder should be dispelled.

Jim Carter was leading the way, ducking under the silk rope, holding it up for Marilyn, and then walking away to the deserted bar at the back of the gallery as Alan followed. Carter's back was stiff; he stumped along angrily, as though unwilling to leave the scene of his partner's battle, and he did not look back to see if Alan was behind. He reached the bar and ordered himself a gin, got another for Marilyn, and then glowered at Alan. 'Yours?' When Alan shook his head, Carter scowled. 'All right, let's take these to the end of the bar. I don't know what this crazy nonsense is all about, but we'd better keep it private, in the family. Come on, over there.'

He gestured with his gin glass to a small circular table at the far end of the bar. Marilyn and Alan followed as he made his bad-tempered way across and sat down heavily in one of the chairs. He took a sip of his gin. 'All right, now what the hell is this all about? Freddy's in there, throwing for fifteen hundred quid, and I'm walking out here for a chat? This had better be good, or I'll want to know the reason why!'

Marilyn glanced uncertainly at Alan, and then sat down beside her husband. 'Alan thinks . . . he thinks that

Jeff was murdered.'

The gin glass was held suspended in mid-air. Jim Carter was staring at it as though it alone had been responsible for his wife's remark. Then his glance swivelled to her, and then in Alan's direction. '*Murdered?* You're crazy!'

'I believe the crash was no accident. Jeff was killed, and the crash arranged to make it look as though he was the victim of his own drunken driving.'

Carter's glance was glassy; he shook his head disbelievingly. 'I can't take that. Who the hell—'

'I was hoping you'd be able to help me prove it. And pinpoint the murderer.'

'But what can I possibly tell you, that'll lead to that kind of—'

'You were there. At Swansea.'

A great roar burst out from the packed floor below them, and the excited babble of the compère reached them across the noise. Jim Carter's glance was baffled, his attention drawn to the events on the spotlit diamond, his mind still confused by Alan Fearnley's remarks. 'Freddy's taken the second match . . . Look here, Fearnley, what the hell are you on about? So I was at Swansea—'

'For some of the time at least,' Marilyn said with a hint of bitterness. Her husband glanced at her in irritation, as though she were introducing another complication into a situation he already wanted to avoid.

'You were at Swansea that night when Jeff died. You were also Jeff's manager. I think there's information you can give me.'

Carter waved a despairing hand, and glanced again down towards the stage and the match between Thomas and the Australian. 'All right, ask away, but let's get it over quickly, and finish this nonsense.'

'I've been making enquiries,' Alan said, 'as a result of statements made to me by an ex-newspaperman called

Edwards. I've spoken also to a bookmaker called Ned Turtle. And now Edwards has been put in hospital by some of Danny Elias's thugs. It all adds up to something—and maybe you can supply the links that'll prove everything.'

'Prove what, for God's sake?'

'That Danny Elias killed my brother when he welshed on a deal he'd made with him.'

The revolving light in the ceiling cast dark shades of changing colour over Jim Carter's features. His lips framed Elias's name, but the words did not come. He finished his gin in one gulp, rose, and went back to the bar, ordered another double. When he returned, he looked grim. 'All right. Let's get this nonsense over with.'

'I want confirmation, first of all, of a rumour that Ned Turtle had picked up.'

'Which is?'

'That my brother had fixed the match with Freddy Thomas that night.'

'Fixed?' Jim Carter sneered. 'Haven't I made it clear to you? Jeff never needed to have any match fixed. He was the top thrower: there was no one to touch him.'

'That's the point. He'd fixed things so he was to *lose*.'

'Against Freddy? What the hell for?'

'Money.'

Carter's tone was jeering. 'Jeff was making as much money as he needed or wanted. And he was heading for the big money—don't you know? The business will pull in maybe three million quid in sponsorship during the next few years. Jeff would've got a slice of that. We all three would have!'

'Even so—'

'Wait a minute.' Carter held up a warning hand, glanced at Marilyn and said, 'I think I know what you're suggesting. The scenario goes like this, hey? Jeff and Freddy do a deal with Danny Elias. They're almost bound

to meet in the final, and if they do, Jeff will allow Freddy
to win, against all the odds. Meanwhile, Danny puts a
bundle on Freddy at good prices, Freddy wins, Danny
cleans up and shows his gratitude to the boys. Aw, come
on! It just isn't on!'

'The information I got from Ned Turtle is that Elias
certainly put a lot of money on Freddy that night.'

'But that means damn all,' Carter insisted. 'He's a *betting* man — and like any betting man, if he sees a chance
to go for good odds he will.'

'But if Jeff was certain to beat Freddy — '

'But he *wasn't*, was he?' There was another roar from
the floor below them and with a hint of desperation Jim
Carter leaned forward, gesticulating. 'Look here, the
odds were still heavily against Freddy in betting terms,
but to a gambler like Danny Elias there was a long-shot
possibility. He'd been talking to me, and I'd told him
some of my worries. Damn it, anyone who knew the game
could see it anyway. Jeff was off form, he wasn't playing
well, he only scraped into the final because of a walkover!
If there was ever a time for Freddy to take Jeff, it was going to be that night in Swansea. *That's* what Elias bet on.
Not a deal, not a swindle with Freddy and Jeff. Just a
straight, form-reading long shot.'

'Which didn't come off.'

Carter leaned back in his chair, shaking his head
angrily. 'And that's a motive for murder? Danny Elias
puts Jeff down because he loses a few quid? You've got to
be joking!'

'The deal — '

'There *was* no deal!' The anger spilled over into
Carter's tone now. 'What the hell do you know about
anything? I was Jeff's manager. I knew everything that
went on in his head? Jeff and Freddy and me, we were
partners — we pooled all the money the two of them
earned, we worked as a *team*: Do you really think that

Jeff, or Jeff and Freddy together, would have — *could
have* — fixed a swindle of that kind without me knowing
about it? No way! If they'd have been approached by
any gambler with that kind of proposition, they'd have
laughed in his face. We three, we were going great guns:
we were sitting on a gold-mine; together, we were going
to milk the game of a hell of a lot of money in a very short
time. No damned gambler like Danny would have been
allowed to get a slice of our action! We were the Three
Musketeers, for God's sake! So there was no way a deal
was on without my knowing. And I'm telling you — I
didn't know of any such deal. And that means *there
wasn't one.*'

Marilyn frowned at the two men. 'This man Nick
Edwards — '

'Now who the hell is he?' Carter jeered. 'Who's this
great source of information? If it's the character Danny
has already told me about — '

'Elias has spoken to you about him?' Alan asked in surprise.

'I've known Danny a couple of years, and I've done
business with him,' Carter explained patiently. 'This chap
Edwards has been bugging him for some time, and if
you're telling me that this cock-and-bull story about Jeff
being *murdered* comes from Edwards, well, believe me,
take it with more than a pinch of salt. I've heard about
Edwards: he's a nut case. He'll do anything to have a go at
Elias . . .' His eyes fixed on Alan thoughtfully. He paused,
as though to make his next words bite home. 'I said
anything — and that'll include trying to raise a stupid call
of murder. Now for God's sake — ' he hoisted himself to
his feet, as the baying of the crowd reached out to them
again — 'let's drop this and get back to the game!'

He drained his glass and marched off across the gallery
and down the steps. Marilyn was staring at Alan
apologetically. She shrugged. 'He's never an easy man

to convince,' she said, 'But if there *was* any truth in what Ned Turtle says, he'd know. Like he said, he was Jeff's friend, and knew everything there was to know. And Edwards . . .'

Alan clenched his fist in frustration. Jim Carter's jeering disbelief had served to underline the doubts he himself had harboured on hearing Edwards's story for the first time: a recognition of the obsessive nature of the ex-newspaperman's hatred for Danny Elias. Marilyn was turning, making her way back towards their table and Alan followed despondently. The fires that had burned in him since he had seen Edwards in the hospital were dampened; he felt uneasy, and depressed.

The crowd was howling; men were standing upright, waving their arms, calling and yelling. Taped music blared in the background: a rousing march. Alan recognized the tune: it was *Waltzing Matilda*. Big Jimmy from the Outback had taken the first of the three legs of his match with Freddy Thomas.

And Danny Elias was no longer sitting at the table beyond the silken rope.

CHAPTER 6

I

'I'll take the bastard next leg.'

Freddy Thomas sat down at the table, his lean, ascetic features glistening with a light sheen of perspiration brought out by the hot television lights. He ran the back of his hand over his mouth nervously; there was a tremor in his fingers that suggested the tension of the occasion was affecting him, however cool he might appear when facing the board on the stage. His cold eyes flickered swift

glances across the intervening space to where Big Jimmy
was sitting, greedily drinking a pint of Newcastle Brown
Ale, and his lip curled as the compère announced, '*You
think he's hyping up with the strong stuff, but I'll tell you
a secret folks, it's just Coke—but now, a few words from
our sponsor!*'

'I'll take the bastard on the next leg!' Thomas repeated,
but Alan was hardly aware of the words as he sat down.
He looked around the room, at the audience settling back
to their drinks after the excitement of the end of the first
leg; the colours drifted across their sweating faces, the
women were laughing too loudly, the men too full of a
falsely based bonhomie. It was all a far cry from the narrow, constrained world of the valley, but just as far too
from Diana and the chicanery of Peter Emburey, and it
was as though Alan was in some unreal fantasy world, cut
away from his roots, suspended in a state of disbelief,
where his brother had been murdered and strangers
brayed meaningless laughter all around him and a sequinned fool cavorted in front of a middle-aged, soberly-
suited whisky executive, while somewhere in the dark
fringes of the room a man who would kill was moving
quietly, menacingly.

'So what happened?' Jim Carter was asking, with an
urgency and interest he had not displayed when talking to
Alan Fearnley.

'It was okay, it was okay,' Freddy Thomas replied.
'That fourth grouping—I got two in the bed, and then,
damn me, there was no way I could slot the third without
a new angle, and those blasted lights were reflecting off
that damn fool advertisement at the back.'

Jim Carter swore. 'You know how Jeff always handled
that kind of situation! He—'

Freddy Thomas slammed his half-pint glass of lager
down on the table. 'It wasn't Jeff who had to place that
arrow! Hell's flames—!'

He was crouching forward, leaning with elbows on the table, and for several seconds his eyes had darkened, as though shutters had come down while he turned his gaze inward, seeking some hidden truths known only to himself. Alan stared at the man, and the first slow crawl of suspicion moved in his mind, but he discarded it, looked around the room again urgently. He turned to Marilyn.

'Did you see where he went?'

'Elias?' She shook her head; her eyes were troubled. 'No. Maybe he's gone to place some bets; he does on occasions like this, to balance the odds a bit. But does it matter? Look, this Edwards chap, are you sure he's . . . well, straight in the head? If Jim says there was no shenanigans over the night at Swansea, well, I believe him. Ned Turtle . . . rumours run through his world, but I don't think we should lend much credence to them.'

For a moment Alan thought he caught a glimpse of Danny Elias at the far end of the room, but two burly men in dark suits were obscuring his view and when they moved, there was no sign of Elias. One of the men turned, and stared in Alan's direction. Then both men moved away.

'It's me to fire first, next leg,' Freddy Thomas said, with some satisfaction. Malice seeped into his tone. 'I'll make that Strine jump, then. And third leg I'll make him suffer, believe me Jim, I'll screw him hard!'

'That's the style, boyo!' Carter said, grinning nervously, lips writhing back from his teeth. He glanced at Alan, as though he considered him responsible for the loss of the first leg. 'You'll take him, Freddy, and then it's all wide open for us!'

Alan hardly heard the words. His glance locked with Carter's. 'Did you see what happened to Elias?'

Carter's eyes were muddy and expressionless. 'So he's left the table. I'd do the same, if you were needling me the way you are him. Leave it alone, for God's sake. I've told you the way it was.'

Freddy Thomas stared at Carter, then at Alan. 'The way what was?'

'Leave it, Freddy, it's nothing.'

'Nothing, hell! I been up there on that stage, firing those arrows, and the least I can expect when you take half my blasted winnings, that you'd be down here taking an interest! Instead, you waltz off with Fearnley and then have the gall to ask me what happened up at the oche — when it's all over!' His mouth twisted unpleasantly. 'I got a match up there — that bloody Strine is on song, and I'll take him all right, but it's not on that I come down for the interval and everyone is needled about something. So what the hell's going on?'

Jim Carter glanced uneasily at his wife, and shook his head in doubt. 'Best leave it, Freddy — we can talk later.'

'We'll talk *now*!'

There was a mean glitter in the little man's eyes; his head was thrust forward belligerently and Alan was reminded again of the cold commitment, the dangerous tension he had detected in Thomas earlier, at the Black Cat and again when he had disposed of his youthful challenger the night Alan had spoken to Ned Turtle. Jim Carter was aware of it too: Alan noted the fine line of perspiration that had appeared on the man's upper lip.

'It's about what happened at Swansea,' Alan said.

The cold eyes moved to him. 'Swansea?'

'I wanted to know what deal you and Jeff had arranged with Danny Elias.'

The thin, narrow lips tasted the word, considered it, then rejected it contemptuously. '*Deal*? What the hell are you talking about? Jeff and me, we had no deal with Elias. What for would we have a deal?'

'Fearnley's got some stupid idea that you and Jeff worked a betting syndicate with Elias,' Carter said hurriedly. 'I told him it wasn't so. Now let's just forget it. We got to concentrate on this match and—'

'No. Wait a minute.' The narrow shoulders were hunched, and Freddy Thomas clutched his darts between angry fingers. He glared at Alan. 'You trying to say there was some fix that night?'

'There's a rumour,' Alan replied woodenly. 'It says the erratic way that game went suggests you and Jeff had agreed Jeff should be beaten, so that Elias could take the punters who had bet on the favourite—Jeff.' He caught the tremor of Thomas's eyelid at the word 'favourite', but went on, 'You both stood to gain a lot of money—or else it was just Jeff who'd made the deal. Either way, the apple-cart was upset when Jeff won the match, after all.'

'There was no deal,' Thomas said quietly. 'Not with me, anyway. I can't speak for your brother.'

'Aw, come on, Freddy,' Carter intervened. 'Jeff made no deal either!'

'I didn't say he did. But I can't speak for him, because he's dead.' The cold eyes turned to Alan. 'As far as I know, that game wasn't fixed. I think I'd have known if it was—I'd been playing with and against Jeff for years. I *knew* him; knew his style; seen him on song; seen him below par. He *couldn't* have conned me up there at the oche—I'd have twigged him early. That's not what it was that night. He just wasn't *concentrating*.'

'He still beat you.' The words were out before Alan could stop them.

Freddy Thomas let out his breath in a low, frustrated hiss. 'Yeah, he beat me. But he had so much luck . . .' He frowned, shook his head. 'But maybe I ought to give him more than that. He was a *professional*. He was off form, and there was something bothering him, he lacked concentration and he'd lost his rhythm, but those arrows were still flying for him. It was automatic; he could do it almost without thinking. So it led to an uneven performance. He still won. But let me make one more point. *I* was in form that night. I could have taken Jeff; I could have beaten him. I was hyped up and he knew it, and maybe that got through to him. But there was always something about my matches with your brother — he could always psyche me down the drain. And maybe he didn't try it that night — he sure as hell succeeded, nevertheless.'

'How do you mean?'

'He was bothered, and it took the edge from his game. He lost control, and so it should have been a walkover for me. But his darts still kept going in — and it took my game away from me. I could have beaten him that night on top of his form — but he was so shaky, I lost my own concentration. What we played that night was rubbish — I tell you, it was *rubbish*!'

The man in the executive suit had stopped extolling the virtues of his company from the stage and the compère was stepping forward again to make announcements about the prizes for the other contestants. In a few minutes Freddy Thomas would be recalled, to fire the first darts in the second leg of the match.

'All right, if you say Elias wasn't involved with my brother in some sort of fixed match, just what was the trouble? Why did the match between you degenerate? What was the quarrel between Elias and Jeff all about?'

'Quarrel?' Thomas shrugged. 'Didn't know they *had* quarrelled.'

'They had some kind of battle in the dressing-room Jeff was using.'

'Where did you get that story from?'

Alan hesitated. 'The doorman at the club — he passed the dressing-room and heard the shouting.'

Freddy Thomas stared unwinkingly at Alan. 'I never heard anything about that. I wouldn't know. But believe me, there was no fix. If either of us had wanted to fix a game, we'd have made it a damn sight more convincing than that. Now can we drop this whole thing?'

Alan hesitated. The theories of Nick Edwards had never seemed less plausible than now, with the denials he had heard from the two men most closely involved with Jeff. He glanced from one to the other: Marilyn's husband, his thick hair curling now, dampened with the tension of the occasion, his sensuous lips nervously compressed, and Freddy Thomas, his lean frame hunched, psyching himself up for the second leg and yet called upon to recall his last match with a man who had died on a windy hillside. They lived in a world that Jeff had made his and it was unfamiliar to Alan. It had its own rules, maybe its own code of conduct, and the undercurrents and the challenges that existed within that world would always be a closed book to him. The parts that twilight men like Danny Elias and Ned Turtle might play were vague and undefined, and perhaps the obsession of a man like Nick Edwards could unbalance the relationships that existed within this private world. As the interference of an accountant with troubles of his own might do, also. Alan glanced around the room almost desperately. There was no sign of Elias.

'All right,' he said quickly. 'So you deny there was any possibility of an involvement with Elias in a betting coup. But that still doesn't cover the quarrel—'

'If there *was* a quarrel,' Freddy Thomas interrupted, 'it wouldn't be that which put Jeff off his game. He'd been odd all week.'

'I don't understand.'

'Something was bothering him; he didn't turn up at the club a couple of days earlier; he seemed kind of tied up in himself, and I knew then my own confidence was building. I knew I could take him.'

'Because he had lost his concentration?'

'In part.' Thomas looked down at the dragon-flighted darts in his hand. 'But I *knew* the Swansea prize was going to be mine. Yet, in the end, he screwed me out of it.'

There had been a sudden, fierce passion in his tone that bordered on hate. Alan stared at the man, saw the tension in his lean muscled arms. And again a tiny suspicion fluttered into his mind, the faint flickering that danced just out of reach even as he grasped for it. 'Did . . . did you know what might have been bothering Jeff?'

'What do you mean?'

'Do you know what he had on his mind — why he might have lost his concentration?'

Freddy Thomas raised his hand, glanced at Jim Carter. Then both men looked at Alan, their interest sharpened by the change in his tone. 'What are you talking about?'

Alan took a deep breath. 'You've not heard of Farrier Enterprises? You didn't know that Jeff had been contemplating a tie-in with them?'

'Farrier Enterprises?' Thomas repeated stupidly. 'You got me lost off.'

'A tie-in, you said.' Jim Carter put one elbow on the table, leaned forward, frowning. 'Just exactly what do you mean by that?'

'I mean that during the week before the Swansea match, Jeff had been approached by a Bristol agency called Farrier Enterprises. They wanted to build him up into star material — '

'He was already a star!' Jim Carter snapped.

'The idea was to pull him out of his present environment, build up his image, and persuade greater sponsorship from the money that's about to roll into the game. Farrier Enterprises would act as his agent, and would undertake all the promotion.'

'And Jeff was thinking of doing that kind of deal?' Jim Carter asked disbelievingly.

'He was.'

There was a short silence. Carter looked down at his hands. 'So that was it. I can see, now, why he's be off form.'

Freddy Thomas shuffled uneasily in his seat. 'What's that mean? What are you talking about?'

Jim Carter pursed his lips thoughtfully. 'To put it crudely, Jeff must have been thinking of a sell-out. It would have meant leaving our partnership, leaving the valley, working with this company — in a sense, letting you and me down, Freddy, when he'd come through the hard time with us, the three of us building together. He'd have thought a lot about that. It would have bothered him, letting us down, leaving Aunt Matty . . .' Carter's eyes flickered to Alan. 'Aye, that'll be why he lost his concentration that week. He was mulling things over; and it would all have been on his conscience, getting him down.'

Alan hesitated. 'Jeff didn't discuss this offer with either of you?'

Jim Carter shook his head, slowly and regretfully. 'No . . . if he had, maybe . . . But he could be a very private man.'

Alan looked at Freddy Thomas. The man's head was down, and he appeared to be thinking, hard. It was several seconds before his head came up. 'No, he never discussed it with me. I never heard of Farrier Enterprises.' But something moved behind his eyes, a half-truth seeking the protection of darkness, and he was unable to hold Alan's glance. He jerked his head, startled, as his name was suddenly boomed out over the microphones. 'I got to go.'

He began to rise but Alan put out a hand, grabbed him by the sleeve. 'Wait a minute, there's just one more thing. You were there at Swansea, till the end. Jim Carter had left earlier . . .' Alan was aware of Marilyn moving uneasily in her seat beside him, but he went on. 'Jeff was drinking pretty heavily that night, maybe morose even though he'd beaten you in the final, still worried, still with something on his mind. But the doorman said he didn't leave alone.'

Freddy Thomas stood staring down at Alan, but his eyes were glassy. 'So?'

'The doorman couldn't see who got into Jeff's car, but someone did. You were there at the club, at the end. Do you know who Jeff picked up, outside the club?'

'So let's welcome them back, again, with a big hand, folks, the man-mountain Australian, the Aussie with an eye like ice, and the fighting bantam-cock from the valley! It's the best of three, and Freddy has always been at his best coming back from the dead! A big hand, folks, a welcome for the gladiators!'

Freddy Thomas tugged himself free from Alan's restraining hand. 'I got to go. I got a match to win!'

'But *do* you know who got into Jeff's car that night?'

Freddy Thomas stopped, turned, glared at Alan. The match with Big Jimmy awaited him, and the adrenalin was surging through his veins as he worked himself up into the state of tension he needed to apply himself to the beating of the Australian. The passion he was thrusting into his blood spilled over into indiscretion as Alan's insistence drew the anger out of him, pushing him into an explanation he was unwilling to give.

'Yes, all right, I know who got into the bloody car that night! You want to know who it was?' He half raised his hand, the darts gleaming between his fingers. 'If you want to know, all right—damn you, it was me! *I* was the silly bugger who got into his car the night he died!'

II

The noise levels had dropped as the tension reached out and gripped the audience by the throat. At the back of the floor supporters still chanted and catcalled, but nearer the stage, where the two men on the diamond could be seen more clearly, the voices were stilled, concentration on the drama being played out before the board now absolute.

Freddy Thomas's face was shining with sweat. The old arrogance was gone, the sneers wiped from his thin lips, and there was no question of his needling the big Australian now, for he was fighting for his life. He had started badly, recording only two hundred with his first two groups, and Big Jimmy had surged into a commanding lead. He had played with consummate skill and consistency, churning out the trebles with an irresistible smoothness. He had stood there impassively, arcing his darts with a barely perceptible flick that presaged complete accuracy, drawing the flights unerringly into their beds, slotting the darts, clear and clean as larksong.

Freddy Thomas, on the other hand, was lurching in his approaches. His early throws had been succeeded by a series that had brought the house to its feet in excitement, but the recovery had been temporary: he was unable to sustain the series and was lacking the consistency displayed by the Australian. He had lost the first game, taken the second with his defiant surge, but was now well on the way to being badly defeated in the third. The big, dewlapped Australian moved up to the oche, twirling his first dart, eyeing the distance and then moving into his ugly, square-set stance. The first dart took the treble twenty yet again, the second followed, and even as the compère brayed—'*There's still a load of room left in the bed!*' the third dart flashed, neatly slotting in beside the other two for yet another maximum.

Freddy Thomas was shuffling nervously, glaring at his feet as he prepared for his next series, and Jim Carter turned an anguished face towards Alan Fearnley. 'What the hell did you want to push him like that for? You've shaken his bloody game and as like as not lost the championship and fifteen hundred quid!'

Alan made no reply. He was staring at Freddy Thomas on the diamond but his mind was full of other images: a dark road on the hillside and the scenario that Nick Edwards had sketched out for him. Jeff had been drunk that night and, big as he had been, he could still have been taken by surprise by the smaller Freddy Thomas. Maybe Nick Edwards had been only partly right, maybe there had been no 'deal' as Ned Turtle had suggested — Freddy Thomas had still had the opportunity to kill Jeff. He had entered Jeff's car — he admitted it. So he could have been the last man to see Jeff alive.

Moreover, he had the motive. For years he had lived in Jeff's shadow. They, together with Jim Carter, had been partners, certainly, but the sharing of money won would not have satisfied the hungers that burned inside Freddy Thomas. He had wanted to be what he could never have been while Jeff was alive: the champion. But that one night, in Swansea, it had become possible. Jeff had been shaky, lost his concentration and the chance had been there for the taking.

Instead, Jeff had won yet again, and Freddy Thomas had been humiliated in the way that young challenger in the New Inn had been humbled. A man could take only so much of that kind of treatment and that kind of luck — especially if he felt, inside, that he had the capacity to win. Perhaps the breaking-point had come for Freddy Thomas that night on the Bwlch-y-Clawdd.

'Hell's flames!' Jim Carter said in disgust as the crowd rose, howling about them, and Big Jimmy punched the air after neatly slotting a treble fifteen and a double top with a dart to spare. The third game was his.

'If Freddy doesn't take the next two games he's lost the whole bloody final — in two legs,' Carter moaned. 'If only you'd left him alone . . .'

Alan glanced at Marilyn. Her face was pale and she was watching him intensely. Their glances locked, and then, with a slight movement of her head she gestured towards the pillars to their right. Alan looked across, and the two men he had seen earlier were standing there. They had been joined by a third. Marilyn picked up her glass, sipped her gin and leaned forward with a forced smile. In a low voice she said, 'I've seen them before. They work for Danny Elias. I'm afraid there's going to be trouble.'

Jim Carter's attention had already reverted to the spotlit diamond. Alan shifted in his chair, his mind racing. It was possible he had pushed Danny Elias too far; Nick Edwards had already suffered for a similar foolishness. Even so, Alan knew there would be no rough-house tactics applied here in the club. He managed a half-smile for Marilyn, to quieten her anxieties, and then turned his attention back to the game.

Freddy Thomas stood at the oche, to begin the fourth game of the leg. His face was stiff with tension and his eyes seemed glazed, but there was a coiled power in his body that had been lacking earlier, a paradoxical relaxation backed with commitment that hushed the audience. He gave his old familiar crab-like shuffle and launched the first dart. There was a rumble of noise, but before it had died he had threaded his next two darts into the board and the compère was calling, exultantly, 'ONE HUNDRED AND EIGHTY! *The match is alight, folks!*'

And alight it was. Even though he was aware of the men standing beside the pillars, Alan was yet caught up in the growing excitement about him as the Australian matched Freddy Thomas's first series with a maximum of his own, only for Freddy, with the advantage of first throwing, to notch up another lead of one hundred and eighty with a beautifully executed maximum. Big Jimmy trembled on his third dart.

'*One hundred and twenty-one*,' the compère called.

Freddy Thomas shuffled in again, leaning forward on

balanced hips, his sober clothing shining dully under the television lights, and there was a surge of cheering as he once again produced a precise treble twenty.

Jim Carter's face was alight. 'Style, Freddy, make it in style!'

Thomas leaned forward slightly, sent his second dart to the board and Alan felt the table rock as Jim Carter lurched against it in his excitement. 'Double twenty . . . no, hell, you've taken the treble seventeen! It's fifteen for the game, Freddy—style, boyo, style!'

The dragon-flighted dart seemed to hang in the air, floating, before it thudded into the board and the room erupted in a vast rush of sound.

'Double fifteen, and it's the fourth game to fighting Freddy Thomas! Pressure darts, folks, but he was out in the minimum three series! So it's Big Jimmy to play: can he sew it all up this time?'

The Australian was rattled; he had been throwing with an unmoved precision in spite of the roars and the baying of the crowd, but Thomas's last darts, with two maximum scores to go out on his third series, had undermined his concentration. In spite of the advantage of first throw, he failed to seize the game: his second dart hit the wire and bounced out, and his third took only a single twenty.

'Eighty! Big Jimmy's let him in here, folks!'

Freddy Thomas was in no mood to let the Australian off the hook. His face was creased in concentration, his eyes hooded against the glare of the lights as he threw his first dart, adjusted his stance to pick up the right angle to achieve the second treble and then, with the bed barred, took a treble eighteen to finish his grouping.

'One hundred and seventy-four!'

'Hold him, Freddy, hold him and squeeze him tight!' The passion in Carter's voice drew Alan's attention momentarily: the man's face was alight as he leaned forward, lost in the excitement of the match.

And Big Jimmy was being squeezed. Whatever the tension on the floor, it was magnified enormously at the oche, and it was getting through to the Australian. A poor first dart brought a sighing groan from his supporters: he struggled through to a shaky treble and then managed a single twenty, but he was shaking his head as he stepped aside to make way for the determined Welshman.

Thomas, Alan knew, was on song again. It was all coming together for him at the right time: arm, eye, distance and calculation, it was all slotting in with his rhythm and stance. The dragon-flights flew, the darts thudded satisfyingly.

'*One hundred and twenty!*'

There were men standing at the back and yelling: 'You can do it, Freddy, you can take him!' The pandemonium was in no manner stilled as Big Jimmy reached the oche. He had to take his first throw against a background of stamping and cheering and he slotted it, with determined concentration, into the treble twenty, but again the pressure was too great and the rest of his series faded. As he stood aside Freddy Thomas said something to him again, and Alan was reminded once more of the young challenger in the pub. Freddy Thomas had regained his skill and his confidence, and he was ready to needle his opponent verbally.

'*Treble twenty . . .*' the compère called and the crowd howled. '*Double top . . .*' The crescendo of sound was deafening. '*And it's treble seventeen to make it one hundred and fifty-one! That's sixteen, double top to go out, and this must be the comeback of the night, I tell you!*'

The dewlapped Australian stood at the oche, shaking his arms, delaying his throw until the tensions eased, until his concentration returned. He lifted an arm, rubbed his sweating face against his sleeve, then, blinking, peered at the board. It was a good series, but it wasn't enough. He knew that Thomas could go out on the next grouping.

They were standing at the back now, some on tables, a few on chairs, waving beer glasses and howling. The din was almost frightening and Alan glanced at Marilyn, but she was swept up in the excitement like everyone else. Alan looked back to the pillars, but there were people moving about there, struggling to get closer to the stage, beyond the silken rope, and he could not make out Elias's henchmen any longer.

Thomas was back at the oche. He stood there and raised his first dart, then paused, turned, and took two steps back towards the big, sweating Australian. His words were lost in the din but they must have been confident, jeering words, because the expletive the Australian mouthed was violent and explosive. Thomas moved back to the oche, his thin lips marked by the confident sneer that was the hallmark of his conviction in his own superiority, and hardly pausing to steady himself he sent his first dart to the board, burying it cleanly in for sixteen. Again he paused, looked back to Big Jimmy, sneering, and turned back again.

The noise died. One dart, to take the second leg, destroy what might be left of the Australian's confidence, and show who was the better player under pressure. The brilliant spotlights blazed down, and the diamond was an isolated island of light, white against the surrounding muted colours; Thomas's wrist was a pale thread poised in mid-air, and it seemed to Alan that the dragon flight, when it left Thomas's hand, almost traced a fluorescent trail as it flicked through the air to bisect the wires, clean and solid.

'*Double top! Second leg to Freddy Thomas!*'

Glasses smashed and tables tumbled at the back as the audience went wild with delight.

He drank two swift halves of lager to replenish the sweat

he had lost, and charge the batteries that he relied on to get him over the nervous tension. His narrow eyes were glittering feverishly and his teeth were almost chattering with the nervous excitement that he had generated in himself and throughout the hall and beyond, for he knew that with the television cameras recording every move on the oche he would be stirring men in a million homes. It was a big night: Freddy Thomas was on his way at last, no longer under the shadow of Jeff Fearnley.

'What did you say to him up there, you confident bastard!' Jim Carter was shouting, slapping Thomas on the shoulder. 'What did you say?'

Freddy Thomas was grinning; there was little mirth in the grin—its foundation was malice. 'I gave him a few choice ones,' he said, 'and then on that last series I just said to him, "Come on, take me on that I can't do it in two. A thousand," I said, and it got to him, and he swore, and I slotted them, got them in two, and I tell you, Jim, I got him on the run, I got him *squeezed*!'

His eyes flickered triumphantly about the table, settled their glance on Alan, and the malice grew suddenly sharper, more intense. 'And I could have done it if your bloody brother had been up there tonight, too! I could have taken him, like I'm going to take Big Jimmy.'

Alan stared at him, angry, confused, disorientated by the noise and the atmosphere and the uncertainties of the situation in which he found himself. Thomas's bitter, sneering triumph was too much to take. He thudded his hand on the table in front of him. 'But you don't have to, do you, Thomas? Because my brother is conveniently out of the way, and you were the last man to see him alive!'

'Fearnley—' Carter was turning on Alan, angrily, panicked, but Thomas slammed his lager glass down on the table.

'What the hell do you mean by that? Are you trying to say—'

'I'm saying just this!' Alan interrupted hotly. 'You admit you got into his car that night. Did you tell the police that?'

'There was no damn call to! They never asked, and there was no reason for me to tell them. Any more than there's reason now to—'

'So you *were* the last man to see him alive! You got in that car, and you drove with him until you were a few miles from home, and then . . . what happened then, Thomas? Did it all go just too sour for you? Did all the frustration of the years, the matches when you were always second best, get through to you? Will you say it was just a drunken quarrel, or will you say—'

'What the hell's got into you?' Thomas's face was dark-stained with anger. 'Drunken quarrel? All right, we were both pretty well away, but there was no quarrel—though there would have been if I could have got my hands on him!'

'If? You were in the car, weren't you?'

Freddy Thomas thrust his suffused face across the table, leaning forward on splayed-out hands as he hissed out the words. 'Not when he crashed, thank God, though I saw it coming the way he was driving! All right, you bloody smart-alec accountant you, I'll tell you what happened that night! I drove over to Swansea with Jim here; Jeff was to make his own way there. I hadn't fixed anything up with Jeff, and when Jim pushed off, as usual, early, to make his call at Neath, I booked a taxi to get me home to Llantrisant, because I had promised to go see my parents. Well, I admit it was a sour night, because I could have taken that championship, but Jeff blew it up in my face! But we were partners . . . there was no quarrel . . . and when the evening finished, and I came out to find my taxi, Jeff pulled up, told me to get in, he'd run me home. And that was that.'

'That can't be the *whole* story!'

Thomas took a deep breath. He glared around the table, at Jim Carter, his face suffused with anger at this continued questioning by Alan Fearnley, at Marilyn shrunk in her chair at the open reference to her husband's visits to his girl-friend in Neath, and at Alan Fearnley, white-faced, disturbed, confused.

'No, it's not the whole story. I tell you, Jeff was just about round the twist that night! Whatever was on his mind, the drink had made it worse, and he was in a funny mood. Kept moaning about his bloody Aunt Matty, and . . . well, all right, I think maybe he did say something about Farrier Enterprises, but I'd forgotten that. But the worst thing was his driving. I was drunk enough, but not too drunk to see the way he was all over the place. We were damned lucky not to pile up before we left Swansea. He just wasn't concentrating: muttering, swearing and blinding, mad as hell and taking it out on me and the road. And that was the way of it right until we reach the Bwlch.'

'What happened there?'

'At the top of the mountain pass the road swings, right down to the valley, left towards Llantrisant. There's a parking area just there, and Jeff pulled in, lurched the bloody car all over the place. Said he wanted a slash. I got out too—I was bursting. And then, suddenly, the bastard left me, just standing there!'

'I don't understand.'

'I tell you he just up and left me.' Freddy Thomas shook his head, reached for another glass of lager already set out for him on the table. 'And I had to walk down to Llantrisant—walk down that mountain road in the darkness! You know how far it is? Five miles and more! I tell you, if I could have got my hands on your brother just then—'

'But by then he was already dead.'

'Now look, Fearnley—' Carter began, but Freddy

Thomas stopped him with a gesture.

'You sound as though you don't believe me, Fearnley,' he said.

'What would have made my brother leave you like that? You must have quarrelled!'

'Any quarrel he was having was with himself,' Thomas insisted. 'I tell you, he was drunk and mad as hell, but incoherent. And when we stopped . . . well, it was all over so quickly, really. He got out first, I decided I'd better do the same. I went to stand by him, and then . . . it was late at night, and there was a car came around the bend, and the headlights lit us up, standing there . . . Well, you know what people are like. He saw us standing there with the futures of Wales in our hands, and the driver, he slowed, and he yelled something, and I was too drunk to make it out, but Jeff, he scrambled back to the car, jumped in and shot off, leaving me standing there! He roared off around the bend and down the hill . . .' Freddy Thomas paused, seemed about to say something and then stopped. There was a short silence. He stared at his lager, then took a long drink. 'That was the last time I saw him, when he went around that bend. And it was a bloody long walk to my mother's in Llantrisant.'

Alan was unable to believe the man. Nick Edwards's theories were still in his mind, and Freddy Thomas admitted to being the last to see Jeff alive. 'Thomas,' he said thickly, 'I don't believe you.'

'I don't give a damn whether you do or not. You asked . . . I told you. Now shove off, I got a match to win.'

'My brother was murdered, and you hated him and you were the last to see him —'

'I said shove off!' Freddy Thomas snarled and his eyes were cold and glittering.

'But we'll do it quietly, sir, and sensibly.' It was the big, heavy man with the curly hair and the cold glance, guardian of the silken rope. Just behind him stood the two men Marilyn had pointed out as henchmen of Danny Elias.

'Now wait a minute,' Marilyn began, half rising in her chair, but the man's glance made her sit down again. His voice was still polite when he addressed himself to Alan.

'Shall we go, sir. *Now?*'

The voice was soft, but the fingers, when they gripped Alan's arm, were like discreet bands of steel.

III

The room boasted a carved oak desk and thick carpeting. The wall lighting was subdued, there was a long, deep settee in one corner, a drinks cabinet in the other and the curtains that screened the long window were heavy and expensive. The room obviously doubled as an office and a place in which the owner of the club could relax.

The owner was not in the room at the moment.

'You have influential friends,' Alan said to Danny Elias.

The bookmaker was seated behind the desk, casually, one elbow on its surface, one hand lightly holding a glass of whisky. Behind Alan stood the two men who had been standing near the pillars; the heavy men who had brought him to the room had remained outside. Elias nodded, smiling slightly. 'He wasn't unhappy about my using his room for a while, provided no blood got spilled on the carpet.'

'This is beginning to develop like a badly-scripted 1940s gangster movie,' Alan sneered.

An edge came to Elias's smile. 'Oh, don't take the situation too lightly, Fearnley. I can be an unpleasant man to have the wrong sort of dealings with.'

'Nick Edwards has already told me so.'

'Nick Edwards!' The smile vanished completely. 'That little nut case! He's been on my back for years, and one of these days I'll *really* convince him to stay away—permanently!'

'So you admit you did have him put into hospital.'

Elias was silent for a moment, watching Alan carefully. Then he sipped his whisky, straightened in his chair. 'Now look, I'm going to be reasonable with you. There's no need for us to get excited about this. You're all churned up about something, you've accused me of having some kind of deal with your brother and—'

There was a tapping on the door, and Elias paused. The door opened, the heavy man with the curly hair apologized. 'Mr Carter—he wants to know if he can come in.'

Elias grimaced, then nodded. Jim Carter slipped quickly into the room. His face was grim, his mouth tight. He ignored Alan after one swift glance, and walked straight up to the desk. 'Danny, this isn't wise.'

Elias widened innocent eyes. 'What isn't wise, Jim?'

'Marilyn is playing hell out there with me, about you strong-arming Fearnley up here. This isn't the way to play things—'

'You got it wrong, Jim,' Elias interrupted, his tone turning ugly. 'I'm not *playing* at all. I've just about had it up to here—' he gestured with his hand at his throat—'and I'm taking no more. Nick Edwards was bad enough, but now if this fool is going to try jumping on the same bandwagon—'

'It's not necessary,' Carter said, shaking his head. 'It's all wild talk, and you've no need to worry. Whatever views Fearnley had, he's already changed them into even wilder channels. He's spent too much time listening to Nick Edwards, too much time accepting crazy theories, so for God's sake don't over-react. If you start twisting arms, the police could get called in and . . .' Carter grimaced, glancing at Alan. 'The fact is, Danny, this clown thinks, first, that his brother was *murdered*, because Nick Edwards suggested so. And that's what it's all about.'

'Murdered?' Elias frowned, glaring at Alan. 'And that talk about the deal I'm supposed to have done with Jeff—'

'He thought you might have killed Jeff to pay him back for breaking such a deal.'

'Hell's bells!' Elias stared at Alan in disbelief. 'And you're the one who goes around talking about bad 1940s films! You think I'd take a welshing that seriously? Break an arm, yes, as a convincer, but *murder*? You must think I'm crazy.' He paused, eyeing Alan malevolently. 'But any character who goes around saying things like that can be dangerous. I'm not sure—'

'Hold on, Danny,' Carter said nervously. 'It's all right, there's no need to take this thing personally. He's already developed other, equally crazy ideas, and they let you off the hook. You'll get no more trouble from Mr Fearnley, I promise you, so just let him go, let me talk some sense into him, and then there'll be no need for the police to go into things, no need for actions of assault and battery, and everything can settle down both in your world, and in mine. So let's just ease it out — Freddy's out there playing in a final, and I've got better things to do than act under pressure from my wife!'

Elias hesitated, glancing from one man to the other. 'You're not making sense, Jim. You say I'm off the hook. What hook?'

Jim Carter took a deep breath. 'I told you, Alan thought at first you were involved in the so-called murder of his brother. That's why he tried to corner you tonight. But after you left the table to set up this little social get-together, he developed another theory. Just as stupid.'

'And what would that be?' Elias drawled thoughtfully.

'I believe he's now decided it was Freddy who killed his brother.'

Danny Elias put down his glass, opened the box in front of him and selected a cigar. He bit off the end, after unwrapping it, spat out the end and lit the cigar, Through a wreath of smoke, he said carefully, 'You got a dangerous, confused mind, my friend — and an even more dangerous tongue.'

Alan remained silent. Carter leaned forward, knuckles on the desk. His voice took on a pleading note. 'Look, let's just forget all this, Danny. No more trouble. This Edwards character, Alan knows now he's talking through his hat. And this idea about Freddy, that's nonsense too. So let's all just drop the whole thing.'

'And this murder idea?'

Suddenly, violently, Carter slammed his fist on the desk. 'Oh, for God's sake, do we have to put any credence in that stupid, drivelling Edwards man? Jeff's death was an accident; the police — no-one — questioned it until this obsession of Edwards's made him point a finger at you. Look, the facts of the matter are quite simple. Jeff had been looking forward to the Swansea match and everything was fine — and then he went off form. I didn't know then, didn't know what was bothering him, what had caused him to lose his concentration, but it appears he'd got an offer from this chap Edsel to strike out on his own. It would have meant breaking with me and Freddy, leaving the valley, his aunt . . . it got to him, worried him, and he didn't discuss it with us so he let it get him down. And that night at Swansea, I saw him play and he was poor . . . but that affected Freddy, and Jeff still won. That was all there was to it. I shoved off then, I had an appointment, but I gather Jeff was pretty down for the rest of the evening, in spite of beating Freddy. He drank hard and I guess the Edsel offer was still on his mind and when he drove home, drunk, preoccupied, he just lost control of the car. That bloody automatic Porsche . . . it was always a bit too much for a ham driver like Jeff was.

But that's all there was to it — just an accident. This talk of murder — it was just Edwards's fevered imagination.'

Elias stared at him, nodding slightly, drew on his cigar and turned to Alan. He waved the cigar in a negligent gesture. 'All right, Fearnley, you lost your brother, and maybe you got your own problems too, coming back home after all these years. Your aunt . . . okay, a disturbing time, but you shouldn't go listening to creeps like Edwards, and these wild stories, these accusations . . .'

But Alan was no longer listening. He stared past Elias unseeingly, as words, suspicions, seemingly unconnected events began to slot into place, sharp, precise as the darts Jeff Fearnley had arced into the boards in a hundred establishments in the valleys. Alan Fearnley had been subjected to tensions that had blurred his vision and confused his rational faculties — the shadow of Diana, the problem of the Sunski fraud, his return to the valley and all the pressures it had brought upon him. But from the moment Jim Carter had walked, surprisingly, into this room, the fogs had begun to clear. Jim Carter standing there in his new 'lucky' suit — anxious to extricate a man he had no reason to be concerned about, finding time to calm Elias when he should have been supporting his partner out there on the stage . . . once a single question was asked, others bubbled to the surface, and the mists began to lift.

'You said you changed your suit out of superstition,' Alan said, interrupting Elias and directing the statement to Jim Carter.

Carter was startled. He shot a quick glance towards Alan, and then turned back to Elias. 'I—'

'And you didn't know about the letter Jeff wrote to Farrier Enterprises. You didn't know he'd turned the offer down.'

Carter snorted in exasperation, and waved his hand. 'How could I? I didn't even know about the deal he was contemplating with Edsel. He never discussed the offer with me.'

'I believe that's true.' Alan nodded thoughtfully, as the pieces continued to click into place in his mind. 'Jeff never did talk to you about the offer. *But someone else did.*'

Silence fell in the room. Carter stared dully at Alan but Danny Elias moved in his chair, uneasily aware of a change in the atmosphere in the room. He growled deep in his throat. 'What's this all about?'

'I've just been thinking,' Alan said quietly. 'I've been trying to work out just why Carter *did* change his suit after that night. He explained it by saying he'd always worn it to bring luck to Jeff and Freddy and that with Jeff's death he had destroyed it, out of superstition. But there could have been another reason.'

'Such as?'

'A man who had taken the wheel of a Porsche, headed it down the hill, steered from the passenger seat, put the automatic drive into third or top to gain speed, and then jumped from the passenger seat to the roadway would have got his clothes muddied, torn. I think that's why the suit was destroyed; and that's why Carter also took a bath when he got home in the early hours of the morning. Took a bath and slept alone . . . until the police called in the morning.'

'Suits . . . baths . . . what the hell are you talking about?' Elias demanded. 'Fearnley, you're beginning to bother me again.'

Alan stared at him. He shook his head. 'Do you know why Carter came in here after me tonight? I'm sure Marilyn *wanted* him to, but since when did he ever take what she wants into account—and with Freddy Thomas playing on that stage in a final? He didn't come in here to get me out of anything; it wasn't even to stop you making the mistake of putting muscle on me. It was to *calm* things down, prevent further questions being asked—because if you'd really put the boot into me maybe I'd have gone to the police, Edwards's theories would have been aired, the whole thing could have been opened up—and matters Carter wanted under wraps might have been exposed.'

Elias frowned. He was uncertain; he felt himself to be exposed in some way he did not understand. 'Jim—'

'Aw, come on!' Carter gave a short barking laugh. 'First it was you, Danny. A few minutes ago he was after Freddy. Now he's going to suggest *I* killed his brother.'

'It's a clearer hypothesis than the others,' Alan said.

'You're making a fool of yourself, Fearnley. I'm warning you—'

Elias held up his hand, silencing Carter. 'All right, Fearnley, your suspicions—'

'Carter couldn't have known Charles Edsel made an offer to Jeff—but he mentioned it to you when he walked in here.'

Carter was taken aback. '*You* told me, earlier tonight—'

'I said *Farrier Enterprises* made an offer. And you said Jeff hadn't discussed it with you. So how come you know about Edsel? Where did you pluck his name from?'

'So the name,' Elias said harshly. 'Why is it important?'

'Jeff had been off form, worried about the offer. That night in Swansea he had a quarrel in his dressing-room: I'd assumed with you, Elias. Couldn't have been with Freddy—he was out front. I guess now it was with Jim Carter. Because Carter had discovered that a man called Edsel had offered Jeff a contract. That made Carter mad as hell.'

'If I'd known about it, I wouldn't have stood in his way—'

'Not so. You had a lot of time and effort tied up in Jeff, and in the partnership with Thomas. It was all beginning to pay off. When you found out about the Edsel deal you stormed in at Jeff. He had already been feeling guilty as hell and you really laid it on him, told him he couldn't break things up this way, he had loyalties, to Freddy, to you, to Aunt Matty—and then he went out, muddled his way through to beating Freddy, and soon he started drinking, hard.'

'I wasn't there,' Carter muttered. 'I'd gone—'

'Yes, as usual, to Neath, to see your girl-friend. But later you saw the Porsche, didn't you, on the mountain road? You saw the car; you saw Jeff and Freddy standing there, and you yelled, slowed. Jeff recognized you; Freddy didn't. And Jeff scrambled after you. What did he do, flash his lights, so you pulled into the lay-by, and then he came in fast, drunk, crashing his wing as he came in behind you?'

Carter turned to Elias. He raised his hands deprecatingly. 'Do we have to listen to this?' Elias made no reply; his eyes were thoughtful, fixed on Alan.

'All right,' Carter said angrily. 'Why the hell should Jeff want to come after me like that?'

'Because,' Alan said slowly, 'I think he'd *changed his mind*.'

There was a short silence. Danny Elias broke it. 'About the Edsel offer, you mean?'

Alan nodded. 'You see, he'd already written a letter turning Edsel down. The decision was a tough one to take—but he'd mulled it over, never cashing the cheque Edsel gave him. He *wanted* to accept, saw the chances he'd have tied in with Edsel, but the old loyalties held him back. He wrote the letter, posted it, probably that day in Swansea. And, still disturbed, still half regretful, but loyal to his friends and his background, he went to play his match. And our friend here went for him. I think Jeff never had a chance to tell Carter he'd turned down the offer: Carter was too mad. And it churned in Jeff all evening. Carter was putting pressure on him when he'd already decided, against his better judgement, to turn Edsel down. And I think Jeff cracked that night. It was why he was so drunk, so incoherent in the car, so repetitive, muttering about Farrier Enterprises, as a half-drunk Freddy heard. And when he saw Carter's car, heard him shout, he went after him, yelling. To tell him that he could go to hell—Carter, the valley, everyone. He was going to take up Edsel's offer.'

Carter stood rigid, facing Alan Fearnley. 'Why are you doing this?'

Alan hesitated. 'Maybe because, like Nick Edwards, I want to seek for justice.'

'There was no murder. I . . . You'll never prove it was murder.'

'I don't intend to try,' Alan said woodenly. 'Maybe in the quarrel he tried to hit you; maybe crushing his head with a stone, or against the rock, was an accident. I don't know. It doesn't really matter. It's all over now. It's all up to the police to fit the case together—the forensic report, your behaviour, your suit, a statement from the woman in Neath about the time you left her, the distance to the Bwlch, the time you got home and took your bath. It's up to them.' He paused, glanced towards Elias. The bookmaker's eyes were fixed on Carter.

'Danny—' Carter began.

Elias reached for the phone. 'You came in here to try muddying waters. You could be trouble to me, my friend. And in my business, there's always someone you can talk to in the police. I think I want to be very clean of all this mess.' He began to dial a number.

Alan walked quietly from the room. Jim Carter made no attempt to follow him.

The sound waves crashed against him as he walked back to the area beyond the silken rope. Marilyn was back at the table. She rose to greet him, looked wildly around. 'Where's Jim?'

'He's still back there with Elias.'

She stared at him, searching his face, but he was staring fixedly at the diamond gleaming under the hot spotlights. The crowd was baying its excitement, stamping, shouting, whistling, and all was pandemonium. Freddy Thomas's face was white and strained and his hair was damp, sticking closely to his skull. Big Jimmy was throwing, and he seemed to have regained his skill.

'He took the first game,' Marilyn murmured, 'and it lifted him. He all but whitewashed Freddy in the second, and though Freddy charged back to make the next two games, they were close. And this, this final game, Big Jimmy has come away with a maximum and two tons, and Freddy's trailing . . .'

Alan turned his head and looked at her. There had been a few minutes on the mountainside when the years had rolled back and he had thought, briefly, that maybe out of the wreck of his marriage with Diana he might be able to create something from past relationships, with Marilyn. But not now. After tonight, it would be impossible.

Marilyn's eyes bored into his. 'What's . . . what's happened? I sent Jim after you . . . what happened in there?'

Alan told her.

She was silent as the noise washed around them. Big Jimmy stood erect, his heavy body leaning forward slightly, and the compère boomed in his microphone, '*And here it is, folks, the first big chance for the title. Big Jimmy to throw, and he needs a clear eye to make it. So here he goes . . .*'

The dart flew, the shout turned to a groan and then a hush.

'*He's blocked now in the twenties . . . he'll switch down below . . .*'

The noise died completely. Alan glanced at Marilyn: her eyes were fixed on the splash of light where the players stood, but he knew she'd be seeing nothing.

'*It's treble nineteen! One arrow, and Big Jimmy can make it for fifteen hundred quid!*'

Alan looked at the stage. The dewlaps quivered as Big Jimmy prepared to throw. Alan looked past the grotesquely large Australian to where Freddy Thomas stood. He was staring directly at Alan Fearnley. But with a prickly shiver to his spine, Alan felt that Thomas was seeing someone else: the man who had always been there to beat him, the man who even in his worst moments, devoid of form, could still humiliate him. Thomas stood under the glaring white lights and his thin face seemed naked in its despair as the ghosts hovered in his mind: his eyes were riveted on Alan Fearnley, whose presence had been enough to maintain the jinx he had suffered from in Jeff Fearnley's existence.

The anguish scarred Thomas's features as the final dart thudded home.

'*It's* DOUBLE TWELVE—*and it's Aussie Big Jimmie's big night!*'

The cameras were panning, the trolley crews moving in as the climactic moments were recorded for a million television sets all over the country; an excited crowd spilled over the tables, scrambling towards the stage; the big Australian, muscled arms raised, was grinning in triumph, grabbing for the bottle of champagne thrust towards him; shouting, cheering, the taped thunder of *Waltzing Matilda* crashing out once more as part of a vast barrage of sound that ignored the slight form of Freddy Thomas, forgotten in the tumult, pushing away to the oblivion of the exit. Marilyn rose as the table beside them went over with a crash. Alan stood beside her; she was trembling.

'I . . . I'd better go to find Jim.'

Alan had no reply to make.

She hesitated. 'You said . . . you said he found out about the Edsel offer. If he hadn't . . .' Her words died, she half turned away. 'Who was it, Alan? Who told Jim about the offer from Edsel?'

'Aunt Matty,' Alan said.

IV

There would be no problems arising out of Jeff's estate, Alan explained to Aunt Matty; it was time for him to return to Bristol, clear a few business matters up, and then look for another job.

She did not question the decision, and he did not tell her of the other decisions he had reached during the last twenty-four hours. To decide that a recall of an old relationship with Marilyn was impossible had convinced him a reconciliation with Diana was equally impossible: their views about marriage were poles apart and the distance was deadly. Then, with his mind clear of Diana, somehow it seemed easier to make a decision about Peter Emburey—he could not countenance the fraud Emburey wanted him to practise even if it meant losing his job. And that, in turn, meant he could perhaps deflect Nick Edwards from the dangerous course of his obsession— Alan would give him material for an exposé of the Sunski fraud that might gain him re-entry to the newspaper world. But he told Aunt Matty none of these things.

And he did not tell her of the part she had played in the death of her favourite nephew.

Her need to dominate, to tie him closely to her had, indirectly, led to his death. Jeff had already decided not to leave her—even though, like Alan, he must have *wanted* to be free, at last. But Charles Edsel had phoned, told

Aunt Matty about the contract and she had rung Carter, sure he would be able to stop Jeff leaving, accepting the offer. Instead, Carter's violent reaction had rankled with Jeff all evening until, finally, on the high road he had made his last rebellion, against Carter, Aunt Matty, and the strangling restraints of the valley existence. But it need never have happened, if Aunt Matty had not made the phone call.

She had still made no reference to that call, though Carter had admitted receiving it. Perhaps, in her heart, she already knew the extent of her culpability; perhaps that was why she now raised no further objections to Alan's leaving the valley.

Her thick-veined old hand smoothed away the non-existent crumbs on the spotless tablecloth. 'You'll come back from time to time to see me, won't you?' she asked.

'I'll do that, Aunt Matty,' Alan replied.

But they both knew he never would.